Burger City Blues

Allan Kemp

ISBN-13: 978-0-9993518-4-0

ISBN-10: 0-9993518-4-2

CHAPTER ONE

The music is too loud, the air is too full of cigarette smoke and the temperature is too low, even considering what a sweltering July day it is outside. I suppose the titty bar keeps the place cold so the girls' nipples will stay at attention. Referring to these strippers as "girls" is a stretch. There aren't just mothers dancing on stage, but grandmothers as well.

You'd think I'd be grateful to have a boss who insists on having our monthly business meetings at a strip club. So, call me ungrateful. This place stinks of stale beer and perfumed sweat. On the other hand, it's the one time I get to talk to my boss, Mr. Earl Bottenberg, alone. Well, as alone as you can talk to someone who's got a beer in one hand, a raunchy cigar in the other, and his nose inches away from a naked woman's ass. It doesn't do much for his appearance, but he quit caring about that some time ago. He was football star handsome until he got what he needed out of life.

I aspire to have what Mr. Bottenberg has and what he has is four Burger City franchises. I don't need four. Not right away. One would do me just fine and then I can grow from there. I understand what it takes to make a Burger City franchise grow and prosper because I've been working for the same Burger City since I was fifteen years old. It's Mr. Bottenberg's first Burger City and still his most profitable. I'm not his first employee, but I'm his only long-standing employee. After fourteen years together, I feel like we're almost business partners.

I would gladly pay to be part owner of the Burger City that I manage for him. It's a position I deserve after fourteen years of working up from scrubbing the toilets to running the restaurant and doing the books for all four. But I can never be Mr. Bottenberg's business partner because his wife would never allow it.

Ah, the vastly strange Mrs. Bottenberg. The strangely vast Mrs. Bottenberg. She who makes these old hag strippers look like supermodels. She's the reason I put up with this monthly headache with Mr. Bottenberg.

She makes his life a living hell, but he doesn't dare leave her. It was her rich daddy's money that paid for that first Burger City franchise. And daddy made sure that his precious daughter had equal ownership. So, you see, Mr. Bottenberg already has a business partner.

Mrs. Bottenberg has stepped foot in any of Earl's four Burger Cities for years. They made a deal early on. She'd get him the money to start his own business and he could run it any way he saw fit. She knew he had the stuff to be successful if he could only get that first big chunk of change. But he was poor and she was ugly. And the one thing in life she truly desired was to be a mommy. Lucky for Mr. Bottenberg, she got pregnant on their honeymoon. He claims he was too drunk to remember it, but I'm not so sure. Every once in a while, he gets this queer look in his eyes, like he's remembering something truly horrifying. Then his whole body convulses violently once, twice, thrice, and then it's over. Until the next time he remembers.

I look up from my seltzer water just in time to see him going through his latest visitation of his honeymoon. The stripper feels his nose making an unexpected lunge to where the sun don't shine and cries out like a kitten in a blender. But then, she quickly regains her composure. Mr. Bottenberg is a regular here at the Feeler's Saloon (their motto is "Feeler? I don't even know her!"). Instead of slapping him silly for touching the merchandise, like she would have done if I'd stuck my nose into her privates, she climbs down off the table and attempts to calm him down. His condition is something the ladies here have been trying to cure for years.

"It's okay, Earl," she coos as she presses his face into her damp cleavage, "It can't hurt you now."

"Thank you, Imogene," Earl replies as he peels his face from her overripe breasts. "I seem to have spilled my beer. Would you be a dear and get me a refill? Besides, me and Randy still have some official business to discuss."

"Sure thing, hon." Imogene chirps as she grabs her skimpy costume and heads for the bar.

Actually, we had already completed our business. I was just waiting for Imogene to finish her table dance before I excused myself to leave.

"Sorry I couldn't make it to the funeral," Earl says. "I had some other pressing matters, you know, that I had to take care of."

"Hey, no big deal." I reply, " Well, I mean, yeah, a funeral is a big deal, but you didn't know Duane that well. Do you even remember him?"

"Sure, I hired him the same day I hired you. You two were quite a team back then. Kept that fry cooker cleaner than anybody ever did and ever has since."

I try to remember that time in my life. Were Duane and I really a team, or even really friends?

"It's funny, the only time we ever talked was when he stopped in at the restaurant. I'm still not sure why Connie asked me to be a pallbearer."

"Connie?"

"Duane's wife."

" Oh yeah, Connie. Well, it's just like I always I told you. Be loyal to your customers and they'll be loyal to you."

What he said was true. The only reason I took the time to talk to Duane was because of this advice Mr. Bottenberg had drilled into me. Be loyal to your customer. Make him feel welcome. Make him feel at home. Make him want to come back and spend more money. My loyalty to Duane was just good business.

"Well, speaking of customers, I'd better be getting back. I'll talk you later, Mr. Bottenberg."

"Damnit, Randy. When you going to start calling me Earl. It's been, what, I don't know how many years now."

" Sorry, Mr. Bottenberg. I'll work on it."

As I pass by the bar on my way to the front door, I stop next to Imogene. Compared to the rest of the girls here, she looks pretty good. Maybe because instead of hiding her age, she wears it proudly like a badge of honor. Must be a country girl thing. It makes you overlook the few strands of gray in her mane of red hair and that her naturally large breasts are starting to sag.

She's being hit on in a very unsubtle way by a cute brunette girl with bright hazel eyes. The brunette is dressed like a construction worker and flirting like one too. I remind Imogene that Earl is still waiting on that beer she promised to bring him.

"And besides," I add, "you don't want to get mixed up with this one. She's nothing but trouble."

"Fuck you, Randy!" says the brunette. "Now give me a hug."

I stoop over and wrap my arms around the petite woman. Kimmie Horenstein is her name and she is one of my closest friends. Hell, she's one of my only friends, since most of my life is tied up working in Burger City.

Many strip clubs in this town don't admit unescorted women; even lesbians usually come in groups, but Kimmie's the exception. She makes a point of being the exception. Whenever I see her, that old David Bowie song, "Rebel, Rebel", goes through my head. Her constant state of rebellion makes her annoying to most people. Feeler's lets her break the rules because it's too much of a headache to stop her.

"Really, Kimmie, you should leave Imogene alone. Aren't you dating Dixie?"

At the mention of Dixie's name, Imogene curses under her breath and hightails it back to Mr. Bottenberg's table with his beer.

"Damn you, Randy!" Kimmie barks as she watches her prey escape. "You scared her off. I was about to get me some fresh poontang."

I know Kimmie likes to say words like poontang, to get a rise out of me and to remind me of what a master horndog she fancies herself to be.

"And besides, I broke up with Dixie last week!"

"Yeah, and you broke up with Willadean the week before," I say. "You need to stop dating strippers who work for the same club, Kimmie. It's bad for your health."

CHAPTER TWO

As I pull into the parking lot of the restaurant, oily smoke is billowing out of the dumpster. Damn punk kids! This happens so often, I don't even bother to try and put it out anymore. The dumpster is far enough away from the restaurant and the customers cars that I can let it just burn itself out. Still, why can't they wait until the weather gets cooler? Why now, when it's already too hot to breath. I let myself in the back door to the restaurant and feel a wave of heat that matches the one I just left outside. The front end of the restaurant is air cooled for our customer's comfort, but back here in the tight maze of high speed cooking machines, there is no relief. It's not the stench of burning grease and overcooked hamburger meat that stops me in my tracks. It's the angry shouting I hear coming from the front counter.

I stride quickly but quietly to the source of the noise. Experience has taught me that rushing frantically into a situation like this only makes it worse. When I reach the counter, a customer is about to explode from righteous indignation.

"What the hell are you people trying to pull here anyway? I paid good money-money I worked my ass for all day in a tight cubicle just so you assholes can rip me off!" he shouts into the face of the young girl at the cash register.

I size him and the situation up quickly. He's short, medium build, thick glasses, crewcut and is wearing a wrinkled blue suit. He looks about my age. Yeah, I know just what he's feeling. The world has kicked him in the nuts and the last thing he needs is a fast food joint to disrespect him by not paying close enough attention to what he ordered.

Then I look at my employee. Her name's Felicia. She's a seventeen-year-old African-American girl who is also my star employee. Her eyes are popping out and she's standing very still. She's a tough kid with lots of street smarts, but this guy has really rattled her.

Last, I take a short tour of my own condition. Standing next to Felicia at the cash register, I can feel some of the draft of the air conditioning. That's good. My car's air conditioning died about five minutes after I bought it. My shirt is sticking to my body from the ride back here and my head is pounding from all the smoke and loud noise I endured at Feeler's Saloon. That little stream of cool air helps me fight down the wave of nausea that I've been feeling since I first stepped inside the building.

"What seems to be the problem, sir?" I say in my best calm efficient manager voice.

Felicia and the customer both turn and notice me at the same time. I can see Felicia's expression soften immediately. Mr. Crewcut is too full of steam to slow down just yet.

"Are you the manager of this stinking grease pit?" He yells in my face.

"Yes, I am, sir." I reply, "We obviously have done something wrong. What can I do to correct the situation?"

He hesitates for a moment. He's trying to decide whether he can get more mileage out of bitching about our incompetence in general or by pointing out what he feels we did wrong in such a way that we couldn't possibly solve the problem without him giving us yards of more shit.

Logic dictates that you choose the latter approach. To carry on without specifics now just makes you look like an ass.

"I asked for no cheese on my burger and a regular soda. I got cheese and a diet soda. I'm lactose intolerant and I'm allergic to NutraSweet. This food could put me in the hospital. That wouldn't look too good, would it? A customer falling dead in your grimy little establishment here, huh? Huh?"

"No, sir, it surely wouldn't," I agree with respectful dismay, "That would not be a good thing at all. Our goal is to make our customer's experience here enjoyable both aesthetically and nutritionally. Obviously, we have failed you miserably."

He can tell I'm laying the bullshit on thick, but he still likes the sound of it. He lets go a little nervous smile and right away feels embarrassed by it. All three of us can feel the tension leaving the room.

"First, may I offer to personally make sure you get exactly what you ordered, sir?" I plead, "And then perhaps you'd be willing to accept a stack of our coupons for free soft drink and an order of regular fries with your next purchase of any of our sandwiches?"

I let him ponder the peace offering. It's the best deal he's going to get from us and he knows it. He shrugs his shoulders and stares at his shoes. I grab his new order and stuff it in a paper sack along with a big handful of coupons. I give him one more apology for the road as he snatches the bag of food and heads out the door.

"Well, there goes another satisfied customer." I said, which makes Felicia giggle.

I think about retreating to my office, but I can feel

that someone is watching me. I hope it's not another lactose intolerant customer choking on a cheeseburger and pointing an accusing finger in my direction. Instead, I see that it's Connie sitting patiently at one of the tables. I always took the time to talk to her husband when he was alive. It looks like the tradition will live on with the widow.

"Connie! What a pleasant surprise."

"Hello, Randy," she says in her little girl voice, "you got time to sit and chat or are you too busy?"

"Never too busy for you, Connie. You know that."

I slide into the other side of the stiff plastic booth so that we're facing each other. We wait until a group of sweaty kids on a sugar buzz race screaming past us and into the attached concrete playground before we try to start a conversation.

"You want some of my fries?" she asks, "I can never finish them."

In front of her are the remains of a City Block. That's what Burger City calls its value meal. It consists of one of our signature Skyscraper Burgers (with or without cheese, depending on your lactose tolerance), industrial size fries and a medium soft drink. It's served in a cardboard box with graphics on the outside that depict a real downtown city block. Our TV ads encourage customers to come in and exclaim, "Gimme a 'Block'!"

"No thanks," I reply as I scan the cold leftover fries, "I had a big lunch."

Connie shyly looks at me with the palest blue eyes I've ever seen on a human being. I would consider them beautiful if she weren't so bland. Her hair is the color and consistency of dry straw, her complexion is as pale as oatmeal, and her features are decidedly plain. Her wardrobe is so rumpled and drab, you can't tell what kind of body she's hiding.

"Thank you for coming to the funeral."

"Thank you for including me. It was an honor."

"Duane didn't have, you know...," she begins, though I'm not sure what he didn't have. Common sense? Good taste? A penis? "...a lot of really close friends...like you."

Ouch. Now, I have to say something personal. I desperately search my memory banks on everything I have on one Duane Schmidt, now deceased. I sat in this booth ("our booth", as the Schmidts put it) with Duane and Connie at least once a month for the past five years while he droned on about their boring lives, but I never retained a word he said.

I searched back earlier to when Duane and I were both fat losers coming here to work after school. And that's when I remembered. The one thing Duane loved back then more than anything else in the world.

"I remember Duane was a huge fan of those Ray Gun Ray movies. You know, those movies about the space cowboy traveling the galaxy fighting alien bad guys and rescuing space maidens in distress?"

"Yes," Connie said. "I know them well."

"Duane had like every Ray Gun Ray action figure and God knows what else. I wonder what became of all that stuff?"

"Oh, he kept them." she replies with undisguised bitterness in her voice. "He kept everything."

"Hey, Connie, I'm sorry if I brought up something I shouldn't have."

"Oh, it's all right," she sniffs, holding back angry tears, "You didn't know. Though, I'm a little surprised. I really thought you and Duane were close."

I don't appreciate her reproachful tone, but I don't show it because I'm the calm efficient manager. Keep the customer happy.

"I'm really sorry, Connie. I thought so too. Obviously, I was wrong."

Connie daps her eyes with napkin. I fight the urge to check my watch.

"I shouldn't have snapped at you," she said. "Maybe I was the only one he shared that part of his life with. He was obsessed with the Ray Gun Ray movies. Whenever a new movie came out, he'd run out and buy all the latest toys. Whatever he could get his hands on. He was a very serious collector. Only the best quality. Had to be in its original box. Unopened. Mint in box. Everything he had. Why would he never open any of it? What was the point? If he loved it so much, why didn't he ever open it?"

She can't hold back the tears any longer. I pull a handful of napkins out of the dispenser on the table and hand them to her. As she cries, I realize she isn't crying about Duane's Ray Gun Ray toys.

CHAPTER THREE

It takes a pile of napkins and repeated promises to come to her house to visit later in the week before I finally get Connie calm enough for her to leave. Meanwhile, my headache grows worse and worse and I can feel the stack of work in my office growing larger and larger. As soon as I see her car leave the parking lot, I dash for the door in the back marked "Private", unlock it, and slip inside.

I sit down in my swivel chair and scan the piles of paper on my desk. Should I first retrieve the large bottle of aspirins I keep in my top drawer or obey the red blinking light demanding that I check my phone messages? Before I can decide, the office door opens. The word "Private" applies to everyone but Mr. Bottenberg and myself. All others must knock first before entering. However, it's Felicia, so I make an exception.

Since fast food server is usually a short stopover in most people's career, I'm very appreciative of the more exceptional workers that come through here. Felicia is one of the best I've ever seen. She's also stunningly beautiful. Tall and athletic with golden brown skin. As good as she looks now at seventeen, you can tell that in a few years she's going be truly magnificent. Right now, the legs are still in that long awkward stage and some of her curves haven't finished rounding out. She reminds me of a young filly that's about to grow into a powerful racehorse. In my mind, I've shortened Felicia to Filly. But I would never call her that to her face because she might find it offensive.

And I would never ever let her know about some of the nifty daydreams I've had of what it would be like to ride this young racehorse. Felicia is one of my employees and she is under eighteen. Sexual harassment and statutory rape are nothing to play with.

"I'm sorry to barge in on you, Mr. Crust." she stammers.

"That's okay, Felicia. What can I do for you?"

I don't ask her to call me by my first name. I prefer formal relations with my employees. Keeps everything in its proper place.

"It's just...it's just..."

"Take your time, Felicia," I say since looking at her is not a crime.

"It's just... I wanted to thank you for what you did for me earlier. You know, with that guy who was so pissed off."

Lately, I've been feeling a real emotional bond developing between us and it scares the hell out of me. It's okay for me to I admire her for her hard work since it's professional respect. But this is bordering on friendship. Nothing bad about that, but I know deep down that my buried lust for her would use this situation to seek something more. I even feel an involuntary stirring in my groin. Maybe if I had some kind of sex life, then this sort of thing wouldn't happen.

"No need to thank me, Felicia. We're a team here at Burger City. We got each other's back. Besides, he wasn't angry at you. He was pissed at the world and we were an easy target."

"Yeah, maybe," she said with a big open smile that sends shivers to places I don't want to be having shivers.

"But that's what makes you special, Mr. Crust. You really seem to understand people."

I feel my face getting hot. She edges closer to my desk and my face isn't the only place I feel hot.

"Do this job as long as I have and it becomes second nature."

"You're too modest, Mr. Crust."

To distract myself, I unlock my top desk drawer and start to rummage for the aspirin bottle. There it is, two weeks old and already more than half empty. Beside the bottle is a heavy shiny metal object. Normally, I don't even notice it, but I can tell by the way Felicia leans in and sucks in her breath, it has captured her full attention.

"Is that your gun?"

Now my face is really hot, but more out of embarrassment.

"Yeah. Mr. Bottenberg gave it to me. He bought handguns for all the managers. Gave us nice leather holsters to go with it. I'm supposed to have it on me all the time, but I don't know. I don't feel like I need to carry it around."

She crosses her arms under her breasts. Her perky almost legal breasts.

"Have you ever fired it?"

"Yeah. Along with providing the gun, Mr. Bottenberg made sure I learned to use it and that I got a concealed carry license."

"Can I see it?"

She can see it fine from where she's standing, but I know that's not what she means. She wants to know if she can touch it. The symbolism of letting her touch my gun is not lost on me, but I put my dirty thoughts aside. I can't see any harm in letting her hold the gun. I take it out of the drawer, remove the bullets, and hand it to her properly.

Felicia grins as she holds the gun. I explain basic gun safety. Don't point it at anyone. Don't put her finger on the trigger. But I can tell from the way she handles the weapon, that this isn't her first gun. In fact, I get the feeling she's been around guns a lot more than me.

I don't know why, but a shiver runs down my back and I think of that old saying that someone just walked across my grave.

She gives me the gun back and I put it away. I wait until she leaves before I lock the drawer.

CHAPTER FOUR

I make it through the rest of the day without any major incidents. I return to the cramped rectangular trailer I call home and do what I do most nights. I surf the net. It helps me think. One part of my brain absorbs assorted bits of information as I wander from website to website. The other part of my brain just wanders.

I admit. My life is pathetic. But things are actually much better than they used to be. My family was poor and lazy. In the hope that I wouldn't be completely useless, my mom made me sign up for my high school's after school work program. She didn't care about the extra credit I earned for experiencing a real job. She knew damn good and well that the program was actually for kids who lived in homes on the poverty line. The money the kids were paid helped their families make ends meet.

Duane was in the program with me, so that's how we ended up applying at Burger City the same day. He wasn't from a poor home. His parents just wanted him out of the house.

Duane and I did hang together back then because nobody else would have anything to do with us. However, shortly after we started working at Burger City, we began to drift apart. For me, it happened one day when we were taking a lunch break.

We were allowed to eat whatever we wanted for free (within reason). We'd both grab two or three Skyscraper burgers and as many industrial fries and then gobble it all down. I was stuffing one of the burgers in my face, feeling the sticky mix of condiments and animal fat ooze down my fingers, when it dawned on me. These burgers were disgusting. They were killing me. Why was I putting them in my system?

I swore off red meat and then anything with a face. I've been a vegetarian long enough now that if I tried to eat meat it would probably make me puke. Duane, on the other hand, stayed exactly as he was; a fast food junkie.

Along with the better diet, I began to get a better self-image. I exercised and bathed more carefully. My excess weight burned away and my face cleared up. Since I was better looking and had some money in my pocket, I was able to get girls to go out with me.

Using Mr. Bottenberg's advice on customer service, I was able to score with almost every girl I went out with. In fact, that's how I met Kimmie. We both used to hang out at Eat Your Veggies, the only vegetarian restaurant in town. I hit on her and she hit back. She was much a horndog as me and for a while we were fuck buddies. This was when she was bisexual. Now she's only into girls.

I was content to roll through life with no real goals, but then Mom casually commented that she thought me and Dad were exactly alike. What scared the piss out of me was that she was right. He avoided ambition like the plague and was happy to spend his days sitting on his fat ass doing as little as possible. When he died, he'd leave nothing behind but unpaid bills. If I didn't want to end up like him, then I needed to find a long-term career goal.

I took a hard look at myself and discovered that I really really wanted to be a Burger City franchisee. Being the manager doesn't cut it. It just makes you hungry to be the owner. And I've got to do this before I'm thirty. After that, you lose your momentum. Your willingness to sacrifice for your goals starts to dwindle. You start thinking about bullshit like quality of life. I'm twenty-nine now. The pressure is on. It's got to be this year or I might as well take that damn gun out of the top drawer of my desk and end it all.

I have all the right stuff to be accepted for a franchise, except the one that counts- $150,000 of non-borrowed personal resources. It's not like I don't save my money. I drive a busted old car. I live in the cheapest trailer home I could find. I never go out because I'm saving every extra penny for that non-borrowed personal resource. But it's not enough. On a manager's salary, it never will be. I need more money. I just have to figure out where I'm going to get it.

I guess that's what keeps most of us going. That endless quest for that certain something that will make all our dreams come true. I wonder if Duane felt like he found his certain something. He never stopped being a fat pimply loser, but maybe he did find happiness. He got married to a wife who thought the world of him. He had his collection of plastic Ray Gun Ray crap. Since he never opened any of it, it must be worth a fortune now.

Just for the hell of it, I check eBay to see what Ray Gun Ray memorabilia is going for on the open market. I'm shocked. Some of the toys are worth a good chunk of change. Nothing close to $150,000 for any one item, but if someone had a decent collection and they were willing to sell that collection, it would be more than enough money for my Burger City franchise.

Connie claimed that Duane was a serious collector who kept all his toys mint in box. Unless he was buried with them, then Connie inherited Duane's collection.

I spend the next few hours doing research on which items are the most coveted among collectors and then I give Connie a call. Hey, I promised her we'd get together later this week.

CHAPTER FIVE

Since neither Connie or I have a life, it's easy to set up a date for the next night. Perhaps date is the wrong word to use here. Connie is a recent widow and I'm a concerned family friend. My goal is to supply comfort to the bereaved and perhaps convince her to allow me to take some useless trinkets of Duane's with me so that I might better be able to remember him.

I'm extremely distracted the next day, but somehow manage to get by without doing anything really stupid. Well, I almost make it. Shortly after the lunchtime rush, Felicia comments to me about how dealing with the huge crowds we get clamoring in here for a quick meal always gives her an adrenaline high.

Without thinking, I replied, "I know what you mean, Filly. I've been doing this for fourteen years and it still gets me a rush."

"Excuse me, Mr. Crust, did you just call me "Filly"?

I almost couldn't speak. Then I answered, "I'm sorry, Felicia. I guess I did. Silly me."

"Is it supposed to be short for Felicia or do you think I'm a horse?"

"Oh, I would never confuse you with a horse. Not that horses aren't beautiful creatures and you're not too bad yourself; it's just that you are obviously not a horse." I gibber before I finally say, "What I mean is 'Filly' is short for 'Felicia'. But I think I'll stick with Felicia from now on."

"Okay," she says, but she continues to look at me in an odd way.

I retreat to my office as fast as I can and spend the rest of the day doing paperwork. The next time I see her is at the end of the business day as I'm heading to my car. She's waiting patiently at one of our outdoor tables for her boyfriend to come pick her up. She has a sack full of leftover hamburgers which is her guarantee that he will eventually show up. I wave good-bye as I steer my car out of the parking lot. I've often considered offering her a ride home. She lives with her mother in the same trailer park as I do. But I know better than to actually do it. It would be a bad move for everyone involved.

I pull up to a stop light about a mile from home. On the side of the road I see Felicia's boyfriend waiting in his sports car while a large boned, sandy blond-haired police woman writes him a speeding ticket. That's the trouble with small towns; you know just about everybody. Felicia's boyfriend, Keith Fleeman, use to work for me at the Burger City. That's how he and Felicia met. He ate more burgers than he sold, which, unfortunately is not enough cause to fire an employee. However, stealing is and he's lucky I didn't have him arrested. However, I did warn Judy Daniels about him and she promised to keep an eye on him. She's the nice police woman giving him the speeding ticket. Well, at least now he has a good excuse for keeping Felicia waiting.

After a quick shower and a fresh change of clothes, I make it to Connie's house in record time. It's a nice little bungalow in a well-kept upper-lower class neighborhood. Duane had made a good living as a plumber. Connie is the bookkeeper at the plumbing company he worked for. It's good that she works. She can afford to keep living here. Otherwise, I might feel guilty for what I'm about to do.

The evening goes well. I take her to the Eat Your Veggies for dinner. It's not too busy tonight or any night for that matter. Vegetarian cuisine is not a big draw in this town. Still, it manages to stay afloat. It's comfortable and friendly and you don't have to kick a hippie to get a seat.

Connie finds my vegetarian lifestyle exotic and fascinating. I keep the conversation light. I purposely avoid talking about Duane. By the time I get her home, we're best friends. I give Mr. Bottenburg a silent thank you for all the clever tricks he's taught me over the years on how to handle people.

She invites me in for coffee and since it would be rude of me to refuse, I accept. We sit in the living room that's been decorated in early American discount furniture store. The heavy scent of potpourri that's been left on the back burner for the better part of a week hangs in the air. Once we're settled in, I slowly start to steer the conversation back to Duane. I never mention him directly. Instead, I keep talking about subjects that would naturally lead to a Duane related anecdote. I want her to think it's her idea to talk about him and his love of all things Ray Gun Ray.

"Would you like to see his toy collection?" Connie said. "It's really something to see."

"Sure," I said nonchalantly. "Sounds really interesting."

She takes me to a small den in the back of the house. Every wall has floor to ceiling shelves, each one full of Ray Gun Ray toys, games, books, models, lunchboxes- well, you get the idea. Each item is MIB (mint-in-box). There's only the slightest hint of dust in the room. I get the feeling that without Duane around, it will gather much more dust than it's ever seen before. The room is a shrine to his obsession. Mentally I pick out as many of the more valuable items I saw on the internet as I can. But there are so many more that I never knew existed that it becomes a waste of time. Here is the foundation of my franchise. I can feel it. Now, I just have to convince Connie to donate it to me.

"I suppose there were times when this obsession of Duane's was a burden for you."

"No, not at all," she said defensively, "He made me a part of it. We had fun doing it together, like an endless treasure hunt."

"But, something was missing?" I venture, hoping I haven't pushed too far.

"Well...," she starts reluctantly, "Sometimes he was so wrapped up in it, he didn't always act responsibly."

I feel like I'm finally getting somewhere.

"Really?"

"Yeah, like when he'd forget my birthday because there was a special edition version of the video coming out. Or like when he rushed to the Target across town in a heavy rainstorm because he heard they were just stocking action figures from the latest movie and he wanted first dibs."

"You mean the one that's coming out this week?"

"Yeah. Ray Gun Ray versus the Cattle Rustlers from Mars starts Friday. It's the eighth movie in the series."

"I didn't realize there were that many. I don't think I've seen more than two of them."

Connie picks up a Ray Gun Ray action figure.

"This is what Duane wanted so badly that he drove through the storm to get it. On the way home, his car skidded off the road, down an embankment, and smashed into a tree. He was crushed inside. But this toy survived in perfect mint condition."

So that's how Duane died. That would also explain why they didn't have an open casket.

"It sounds stupid, but I almost wrote the movie studio a letter," she said with tears welling up in her eyes, "To tell them that they were responsible for my husband's death. The movies aren't even interesting anymore. Haven't they made enough money off this franchise?"

I see that it's time to find out if my plan will work.

"Connie, it would seem to me that seeing these reminders of Duane's obsession are interfering with the happier memories you have of him. Perhaps I can be of help." She looks at me hopefully. "I'd be happy to take all of Duane's collection off your hands. In fact, I'd be willing to pay you whatever you think is fair."

If she knows their true market value then I'm shit out of luck.

"No, Randy, I couldn't. As painful as this collection is to me, this is Duane. And until I'm ready to let him go in my heart for someone new, then I must keep the legacy he left behind. And besides, I'm not sure you could afford it. This stuff is actually worth a lot of money."

"You're right." I said trying to hide my disappointment. "I hope you I wasn't out of line."

"Oh, heavens no!" she said with an unexpectedly

bright smile, "You've been so sweet. In fact, let me make show how much I appreciate your kindness by making you a home cooked meal. Believe it or not, I'm a very good cook!"

I almost refuse, but then that goofy old saying goes through my head about the way to a man's heart is through his stomach. Could it be that while I've been trying to get something from her, she has been trying to get something from me? Maybe this deal isn't dead yet.

CHAPTER SIX

I'm back home surfing the net. Maybe somewhere in this endless ocean of electronic data I can find the answer to my dilemma. I want Duane's Ray Gun Ray collection. His widow, Connie, owns it and won't give it up. She knows it's valuable, but refuses to sell it because it reminds her of Duane.

However, I got the impression she might be talked into giving it up to someone she felt close to. Someone like me, maybe. I definitely got the signal that she wants me. For what exactly, I'm not entirely sure. Though she hinted that her sex life with Duane was less than satisfactory, I seriously doubt that she wants to have sex with me. Duane's been in the ground for less than a week.

On the other hand, I really need that collection. Some of the items I saw in Duane's room weren't mint in box but were displayed in glass cases. They appeared to be unfinished toys. I look them up and discover that they're prototypes for figures that were never made.

I lurk around Ray Gun Ray chat rooms and casually mention these prototypes. It causes a flurry of excitement. Seems Duane was sitting on a regular Holy Grail of Ray Gun Ray memorabilia. Hard-core collectors would give their left nut for those dull chunks of plastic.

So, does this mean I'm willing to befriend his poor widow just to get my hands on his collection? Am I really willing to be that deceptive? You bet your sweet ass I am! But what if she really does want to jump my bones? What if she needs somebody to love her in a way that Duane was never able to do. He couldn't. He was already in love with his precious pile of colored plastic. And if our relationship only lasts until I'm able to convert that pile into my Burger City restaurant, then at least she gets to walk away feeling she finally experienced something in her otherwise bleak empty life.

The thing about Connie that I picked up on right away is that she's a cipher. Look into her head and there's nobody home. That is, until somebody puts something there. She has no direction of her own, so she waits until someone comes along and gives her one. However, Duane's death made her wary of going in just any direction, so I'll have to be extra charming. Plus, I don't' want to go too far and find myself trapped like Mr. Bottenberg. The only marriage I want right now is to a Burger City franchise.

A knock on the front door of my trailer home makes me jump. I glance at the clock on my computer screen. It reads 10:32 PM. A bit late for visitors, but I never have visitors. I'm sitting at my desk chair in nothing but a pair of shorts and sandals. The window unit air conditioner in the bedroom keeps that room cool so I can sleep. It only manages to keep the rest of the trailer from becoming a complete oven. I would put on a shirt to greet my mystery guest, but it seems too much bother. Actually, I'm hoping they went away, when the knocking starts up again. So, I get out of my chair and open the door.

Standing on my front stoop, illuminated by a bare bulb hanging above her head, is Felicia. She's wearing a T-shirt and a pair of gym shorts. The T-shirt is so old that whatever was written on the front is faded to complete obscurity. She outgrew it some time ago. It's so tight I can not only see that she's not wearing a bra, I can also clearly make out the outline of her aureoles. She must have gotten the gym shorts the same day she got the T-shirt because they're equally as tight. Camel toe is not always a bad thing. If for no other reason than to stop myself from staring at her, I throw the door open and invite her in. She takes two confident steps inside, since three steps would run her into a wall.

"I'm sorry to bother you so late. Were you sleeping?" she asks.

I still can't believe she's physically inside my home. The mannish mess surrounding us makes me feel more naked than not wearing a shirt. But I force these thoughts away and respond, "Oh no. I was doing some stuff on my computer."

"Good," she said. "So, I guess you're wondering why I'm here."

"If it's about a raise, I'll do what I can, but I can't make any promises."

"No. It's not that. Can you can give me a ride home from work tomorrow?"

"Sure, no problem."

Since she normally gets a ride home with her boyfriend, Keith. When I saw him pulled over by the police, I thought he was just getting a speeding ticket. Maybe he's in deeper legal trouble than a traffic violation and that's why he can't take Felicia home.

"Mr. Crust, can I ask you a personal question?" Felicia said.

"Sure, you can ask me. But I might not answer." she frowns at this, so I add, "And since we're here in my home, why don't you call me Randy," which earns me a smile.

"How much money do you make as a manager?"

"I don't wish to reveal the exact figure, but I do pretty good." I can see the next question coming, so I head it off at the pass, "But, you wouldn't believe it looking at how I live."

"Sorry to be so nosy, but you see, I'm not working my butt off at Burger City just so I can live in a trailer home forever. I've got ambition. I'm thinking I might to be a manager someday. But, if it doesn't get you beyond this" she said waving her hands to indicate my home, "Then what's the point?"

"The point is, don't use me as an example," I said, "Most of what I make goes into savings." She gives me a look that says she'd like more explanation. "Your ambition is to become a manager. My ambition is to be an owner. I'm saving up to get my own Burger City franchise. "

To my surprise, her face lights up. It's as if my ambition turns her on. I swear I can see her nipples get hard. She moves a little closer toward me. I need to cool things off.

"Why do you need a ride home?" I ask. "Something wrong with Keith's car?"

Her shoulder's sag.

"Keith and I broke up. He was cheating on me."

Keith is a big guy with big tastes. And he's stupid. But I didn't think he was stupid to cheat on a girl like Felicia. Again.

He was a football hero in high school, which only affords you a few years of glory once you graduate. He's been riding the last fumes of that glory for a while now. He flunked out of the local Junior College and real college wasn't even an option. The few jobs he tried to hold, he's either been fired from or just didn't show up. He drives a fancy sports car and lives in a nice apartment, but it's all paid for by Mom and Pop Savings & Loan. He's too stupid to realize that his time is running out.

Despite all that, there's only two things about the guy that I can't stand. The first is he has no chin. If God didn't see fit to give you a chin, then he must not like you very much. And if God doesn't like you, then, why should I? The other reason I hate him is because of all the times he's hurt Felicia. And this time is the worst of all.

"I can't believe it. How could he cheat on you?"

"I don't know," she said, tears starting to fill her eyes, "All this time I thought he loved me."

"He's a fool. A damned fool. Only a damned fool wouldn't be grateful to be with you and you alone."

She takes an awkward step towards me and holds out her arms. Without stopping to think, I open my arms and she wraps hers around my waist. She cries on my bare chest.

I should only be thinking about comforting her, but the sweet fragrance of her hair fills my head. Her firm breasts press against my bare stomach. I'm starting to get an erection. If we don't stop holding each other soon, I may not be able to control myself.

I try to gently pull away so that I might offer her something to drink. Then I can retreat to the other room to recover. But she clutches me tighter. I stand very still. She slowly grinds her hips against me.

"How old do you think I am?" Felicia said.

"Seventeen," I said.

"I'm actually nineteen. My mother lied about my age so she could keep getting welfare money for me."

I look down into her large brown eyes.

"Why are you telling me this?"

I can feel us both turning into liquid as she presses her lips against mine and snakes her tongue down my throat. There are other reasons not to do this, but she just removed the biggest obstacle.

I don't remember taking off our clothes or getting in my bed. But I remember everything else down to the smallest detail.

Afterwards, as we lay curled up together, feeling the cool breeze from the air conditioner blow away the last waves of steam rising from our bodies. I can't stop staring at her. She is the magnificent racehorse I imagined her to be. She's also my employee. I'm totally screwed.

"Don't worry, Randy," she said, "I won't tell anybody at work. It will be our little secret." Wow, she's a mind reader too. Is there nothing this girl can't do? "Look, I came on to you. I was hurt and angry about Keith and I made a play for you. And also, I really like you."

"I really like you too, Felicia, but..."

"You know, when we're alone, you can call me Filly if you want to."

Can I really trust her? Then again, what does she have to gain by lying to me? If she was telling the truth about her age, then there's nothing wrong about what we did. I really shouldn't have sex with an employee, but it's not illegal. Maybe I should just accept this good fortune and stop worrying.

"Okay...Filly."

CHAPTER SEVEN

The rest of the week I do a balancing act in my head. On one hand, I try to figure out the best way to seduce Connie into giving me Duane's Ray Gun Ray collection. On the other hand, I try not to treat Filly any differently at work. It doesn't help that every time I look at her, I think about what we did and if there's a chance we might do it again real soon. Calling her Felicia instead of Filly might help get my mind off her, but I keep slipping up. And on top of all this, Mr. Bottenberg keeps popping in and he never pops in.

He stumbles into my office, his face grayer and his breathing more ragged than usual. I mention this to him and suggest that maybe it's time to quit smoking those rancid cigars he loves.

"If only that was the problem," he said, then spits brown gunk in the trashcan, "But it's much worse than that."

He leans across my desk and grabs my wrist. His eyes are watery and his hand is clammy cold.

"She wants another one!" he said and now I can clearly see the horror in his face.

"You don't mean...?" I ask, my spine a frozen rod of ice.

"Now that Earl Jr. is all grown up and about to go off

to college, she's getting that empty nest feeling. She wants to have another child...with me!" he said with genuine surprise. "I've managed to talk her into waiting until Earl Jr. moves out in September. You know, so that there's no chance he'd walk in on us."

"Yeah. You wouldn't want that."

"That's just a little over a month from now. What do I do?"

"Don't panic, Mr. Bottenberg. We'll think of something."

"Thank you, Randy. I knew I could count on you. I don't know what I'd do if you ever left Burger City."

CHAPTER EIGHT

Driving home tonight, my head is full of bees buzzing around and stinging my brain. If only I could solve one of my problems, maybe it would make the others more manageable.

"You mad at me?" asks Filly.

I didn't mean to ignore her. I've been driving her home for a week now and we usually talk for the entire drive.

"I'm sorry, Filly." I shrug helplessly. "I just have a lot on my mind these days."

She puts her hand on my knee.

"Maybe I can help you get your mind off your problems."

I grin like an idiot.

"If it hadn't been for you, I would totally be losing my shit these days."

She gives my crotch a friendly squeeze before pulling her hand away. We spent the last week becoming very familiar with each other's body.

"Are you worried about your date with Mrs. Schmidt?"

I cringe. I still can't believe I told her about it.

"You're not jealous or worried about it," I said. "Are you?"

Filly laughs.

"Naw. I'm not the jealous type. Besides, we just fuck buddies. If you want to go out for some strange trim, that's your business. I might just step out too."

Now I'm the one who's jealous.

"It's not a date," I said. "It's a business meeting."

"What sort of business will you and Mrs. Schmidt be conducting?"

It's not that I don't trust Filly, but my plan seems so bizarre. I can't tell her that I'm trying to seduce a widow into giving me her dead husband's toys.

"Mrs. Schmidt has some items that I'm going to liquidate for her. I'll charge her a commission which I'll add toward the down payment for my franchise."

"Really? What kind of items? Jewelry? Artwork?"

I'm taken back by the tone in her voice. There's a hunger there.

"She asked me to keep this confidential," I said. "You know how it is."

"Yeah," Filly said as she looks out the window. "I know how it is."

She doesn't say anything else the rest of the way to the trailer park. Somehow, I hurt her feelings, but there's nothing I can do about it. I have to keep this to myself.

I park in front of my trailer and wait for her to get out. Instead, she leans over and kisses me.

"What are you doing for dinner?" she said.

"I don't know," I said. "I haven't thought about it."

"Because you're what I want for dinner. What do you say?"

It takes a few moments for the blood to stop rushing to my head.

"That's funny," I said. "You're what I want for dinner. And dessert."

CHAPTER NINE

Saturday night arrives with me standing on Connie's doorstop, just late enough and just dressed up enough to be fashionable. She comes to the door wearing a checkered granny apron over a simple ankle length, floral print rayon dress. She invites me in, but then immediately excuses herself to take care of a minor cooking emergency in the kitchen.

I step into the living room, bracing my nostrils for another attack of over-cooked potpourri. Instead, I'm delightfully surprised by the enticing smells coming from the kitchen. I wonder sadly if it's anything I can actually eat. Connie refused to discuss tonight's menu. Few non-vegetarians really understand our dietary requirements, so I suspect I'll have to have my real dinner when I get home tonight.

Soon, Connie joins me in the living room, sans granny apron. The dinner is under control and ready to serve once we're settled at the table. She's all giggly and bubbly with nervous energy. It's annoying, but I manage to remain charming. Taking deep breaths, I follow her into the dining room.

I'm pleasantly surprised by what I find. On the dining table and side tables are candles of various sizes casting flickering shadows on the walls. Van Morrison plays at a tolerable volume from a CD player in the corner of the room. Waiting patiently is a bottle of merlot wine of midrange quality. The room reeks of elegant romance. I'm too speechless to comment. Instead, I do the proper gentleman routine and hold her chair, then pour us both a generous glass of the wine.

"I have a confession to make," she said, after taking a dainty sip from her glass. "I've been spying on you."

I choke on my wine, but quickly recover.

"Really," I said.

Connie giggles.

"I wanted so much to surprise you with a dinner you could enjoy. You know, being a vegetarian and all. So, I went down to Eat Your Veggies and snooped around." She takes a more generous sip of wine. "I asked them where I might find some good vegetarian cookbooks. And since you were a regular there, I asked them if they knew what kinds of things you liked in particular. Well, as luck would have it, a good friend of yours happened to be in the restaurant at the time and overheard me talking."

"A good friend of mine?"

"Yes. Kimmie!"

"Kimmie? You talked to Kimmie Horenstein?"

"Oh yes! She was soooo helpful." she said, getting high from the combination of wine and having center stage, "She told me where to search the web for some great vegetarian recipes. She told me what kind of music you like and what kind of wine you drink. She even suggested the candles. Aren't they romantic?"

"Why?"

"I dunno. Because of the way they give the room light, but still keep it dark at the same time?"

"No, Connie," I said, trying to keep my voice calm, "Why did you do all this?"

"Well," she said, her face taking on the characteristics of a cornered rabbit, "I just wanted to make sure everything was perfect. I like to make people happy. It's what I do. Make others happy. Nothing in particular makes me happy, so if I can make somebody else happy, then I'm happy."

I give her my most sincere smile.

"Well, you sure made me happy, Connie. This is wonderful!"

The look of relief on her face is immense. She slips back into her giddy hostess mode and serves dinner. The dishes are so good, I'm tempted to rub them on my chest.

"You are an artist, Connie, a real artist," I said. "Everything is amazing."

"Oh, stop it," she replies, her face turning bright pink, "It's just a hobby."

"But one you obviously are very passionate about. I can tell."

"Yes, you're right. I never thought about it before,

but you're absolutely right. I love to cook. I love learning about different types of recipes and making up some of my own. I guess it's a hobby to me the same way collecting toys was to Duane."

I let that one go. Now is not the right time to pursue Duane's collection. The stage hasn't been set yet.

"You know, Connie, you have to wonder. Here we are, two people who really have no business ever being in a fast food restaurant. But, instead I manage one and you eat there on a regular basis. How crazy is that?"

"Maybe we should get together and open a vegetarian restaurant."

"Sadly, this town's barely big enough for Eat Your Veggies to stay in business. No, I'm afraid the fast food junkies far outnumber us."

"What's your hobby, Randy?"

Stealing from widows and sleeping with my employees? No, better save that one for later. Better to stick with the most charming and harmless response.

"I dunno, Connie. I guess I'm like you in that my hobby is to make people happy. It's what I do."

"You know what would make me happy?" she asks, blushing while pushing her face into her sleeve.

"Tell me. Your wish is my command."

"I wish you would make love to me."

I don't move. I don't speak. The room suddenly feels very warm and I can feel the sweat running down the side of my face.

"But Connie," I finally manage to say, "What about Duane?"

"Duane's dead. You should know. You were at his funeral."

"Yeah, but that was like two weeks ago. Shouldn't you still be in mourning?"

"I went in mourning for Duane a long time before he died." she said angrily, "Look, Randy. I know I'm crazy to ask you but I really need this. You don't have to pretend you're attracted to me. I just don't want to spend another night alone. And now with Duane gone, I shouldn't have to."

Let's face it. Having sex with a recent widow is in bad taste even if it's her idea. A better man than me would have refused. But I was impressed. And flattered that she chose me. She's not much to look at, but I can work around that. It's amazing what a man will do to get his hands on a never released to the public Ray Gun Ray prototype action figure.

CHAPTER TEN

I'm standing naked in Duane's den, staring at the floor to ceiling shelves of Ray Gun Ray collectables on the walls while trying to focus. I must focus. Upstairs in the master bedroom, Connie is snoring. Not loud enough to be unladylike, but steady enough to keep me awake.

What can I say about what I just experienced with her? First let me say that the sex was incredible! In an effort to impress her, I decided to brush off some of the cleverer sexual techniques I'd learned over the years. Her curiosity was so immense that she went with everything I tried, and invented a few new wrinkles along the way. What's more, it turns out that under all those baggy clothes, she's been hiding a nice luscious body with large breasts and generous curves. Her skin is the color of cottage cheese, but you can't have everything.

As great as the sex was, it lacked the inner passion I felt with Filly. If we had made an emotional connection, it would have added to the confusion I feel now. Here's the problem as I see it. I could easily keep this up with Connie indefinitely. I could make her my girlfriend and have great sex all the time. It would make getting Duane's collection much easier. But it would be wrong.

I don't mean that it would be wrong because I don't love her and I would be taking advantage of her and all that moral crap. Wrong because I'd have extra baggage on this deal that I just can't afford. I must stay focused on my goals. I must remember what it is I want. I want Duane's collection so that I can sell it and use that money to get my Burger City franchise. Anything or anybody else will just get in the way. So, focus. Duane's collection. Burger City franchise. Yeah.

CHAPTER ELEVEN

Things are going great. My birthday is just two months away, but I can feel it in my bones that I'm actually going to pull this thing off. I'm screwing Filly and Connie on a regular business. I've never gotten laid so much in my life. I've managed to convince Filly that my relationship with Connie is strictly business and I've managed to convince Connie that we were meant to be together. She hardly even mentions Duane and seems to have forgotten about his toy collection.

I even came up with a solution for Earl.

"Tell Mrs. Bottenberg to wait a year," I told him. "Just to make sure Earl Jr. doesn't decide that college isn't for him and wants to come live at home."

"That's a great idea!" Earl said. "And the best part is, that's probably what's going to happen anyway. That boy is dumber than a bag of hammers. He'll come running home to mommy in no time."

We're having our monthly business meeting at Feeler's Saloon. Imogene sits next to Earl. She is doing her nails. I am about to leave so she can start shaking her ass in Earl's face when we hear yelling at the bar. Imogene dashes over there. Earl and I look at each other and shrug our shoulders.

Imogene comes back laughing.

"Dixie and Kimmie are having a fight," she said.

"What did Kimmie do this time to break Dixie's heart?" I said.

"She came in with her new girlfriend. Bad enough that she's seeing Connie on the side, but she didn't have to rub it in Dixie's face."

I feel an icy chill run down my spine. Certainly, Kimmie's Connie couldn't be my Connie. I rush over there to make sure. My heart sinks when I see Connie Schmidt cowering at the bar while Kimmie and Dixie scream in each other's face.

The manager escorts both women out of the bar. Connie follows them. I don't think she even saw me. But I feel like I just watched Duane's toy collection leave with them.

CHAPTER TWELVE

My footsteps make crunching noises as I walk across Feeler's Saloon's gravel parking lot. I've never been here at night so this is the first time I've seen their multicolored neon sign all lit up and buzzing against the hazy night sky. There's a pink outline of a very shapely woman with her eyes closed. As a green hand reaches behind her, her eyes open and her mouth changes from a sleepy red lipstick smile into a hard-round circle. This little transaction between woman and hand cycles in time with the words "Feeler's Saloon- First Class Live Nude Girls". I understand every part of the sign, except the green hand. Are we to assume that aliens come here to cop a feel?

But I'm not here to contemplate the sign. I'm here to see Kimmie. I have to find some way to convince her to stay away from Connie long enough for me to get Duane's toy collection. After that, she can Connie. In fact, it will make my life easier if she did take Connie off my hands. But only after I get the toys.

I know Kimmie is here. She's here every night.

You won't find Mr. Bottenberg or Imogene here at night. We only do business at Feeler's during the day. It's an entirely different crowd here in the evening. It's louder and reeks from the sweat of desperate men.

I find Kimmie sitting at her usual spot at the bar. I guess the manager forgave her for causing a ruckus earlier that day. She's sipping a Long Island Ice Tea and flirting with a dancer I've never seen before. The dancer is a tall peroxide blond with large manufactured breasts, a slim waist and sticklike legs. Her baby blue shimmering see-through nightie has long lost its shimmer and hangs dejectedly down to the tops of her thighs. Her face has weathered too many disappointments to hide with makeup, but she makes the effort anyway. Kimmie is wearing khakis and a navy-blue oxford shirt, which just so happens to be what most of the men in the bar are wearing.

There is an empty stool next to Kimmie. I grab it before anyone else can claim it. Kimmie greets me with a big smile and a friendly kiss on the cheek. She gets the bartender's attention for me and I order a draft beer. We make small talk while I wait for my beer to arrive. I pay for it and then take a slow smooth sip. Even with the air conditioning going full blast, the crowded mix of teasing estrogen and frustrated testosterone has driven the humidity up in the room beyond the comfort level. The ice-cold liquid brings welcome relief.

I'm close enough to Kimmie that we don't have to shout, but we still have to talk louder than you would in a regular conversation. She brings up the subject of Connie before I get a chance to.

"When did you start sleeping with Connie?" she said.

"I was going to ask you the same question."

"Normally, I wouldn't care who is bumping uglies with the people I am bumping uglies with, but I'm in love with Connie."

I stare at Kimmie.

"Are you shitting me?" I said.

"I'm serious as a heart attack. I never thought I'd fall this hard for anybody. That's why I brought her here. So, I could let Dixie know that it was over between us."

"You can't be in love with her."

"Why not?"

"Because I'm in love with her."

I had to say something. Besides, I didn't believe Kimmie was really in love with Connie. What she loved was causing problems as only a rebel can do. On the other hand, Kimmie may be the most stubborn person I've ever met, but deep down she has a good heart. For her, part of being a rebel also means being noble. It'll win out over her libido every time.

"Does Connie know how you feel about her?" Kimmie said.

I look at my shoes in an aw-shucks way.

"I haven't gotten the nerve to tell her yet. I was afraid it might be too soon. You know, since Duane died."

The dancer Kimmie was flirting with, who had been listening to us talk in a bored detached way, mumbles something and then waddles toward the cigarette machine. Along the way, a big hairy arm reaches out and grabs her like the green "alien" in the neon sign. Only attached to this arm is a tall beer-belied man wearing worn jeans, a brand-new flannel shirt and tan work boots. He's sitting at a small table with three other guys of similar size and dress. He offers the dancer a ten-dollar bill for a table dance. She glances back at Kimmie, then shrugs her shoulders. He helps her onto the table top and then sits heavily back in his chair as she begins to disrobe to the rhythm of the music blasting from the speakers.

As Kimmie watches her dance, she says to me, "I'm sorry, Randy. I had no idea. She does talk about you a lot. I probably didn't see what was going on with you two because I didn't want to see it." She squares her shoulders. "I won't stand in your way."

"Thank you, Kimmie. You're a true friend."

We spend the next hour drinking beer and arguing about which dancer has the best tit job. The blonde dancer rejoins Kimmie. I use her arrival as an excuse to leave. After a quick round of good-bye kisses, I detour to the men's room for a long piss before the drive back home. As I'm standing in front of the urinal relieving myself, I can feel someone staring at me. Over in the corner of the yellowed tiled room, Filly's ex-boyfriend, Keith, is glaring at me from another urinal. He's very drunk and his angry stare keeps veering off course. I finish up and hurriedly zip up my pants. He's still pissing as I head out the door.

The crisp night air is a welcome friend as I make my way across the parking lot. I parked under a street light, so my car is spotlighted. It feels like an oasis when I reach it. However, the rest of the parking lot is dark. I can't see if I was followed, but anybody can see me. I should get in the car and drive away as fast as I can. Instead, I stand frozen with my hand on the door handle, listening for the approach of footsteps.

I smell the alcohol steaming from his pores before I see him. Keith seems to materialize out of dark into my circle of streetlight. His clothes are rumpled and soaked in sweat. He stops about two steps away from me, weaving from side to sides.

"You took my girl!" he said in a whiny growl, "I want her back."

"I don't know what you're talking about, Keith. Go home. You're drunk."

"Don't you tell me what to do!" he shouts, waving his finger at me, "You do what I tell you, Mr. Burger City. You stay away from my girl."

He stumbles back a step and I think he's about to fall. Instead, he spins around and throws his fist into my jaw. The impact throws me against my car. I'm angrier at myself for letting an idiot drunk tag me so easily than in pain from the punch. For my own self-respect, I swing my fist straight into his nose. Then I immediately rub my hand against my pants to wipe away the ache in my knuckles and the nasty sweat and blood from his face. Keith takes another unsteady step backwards and this time he does fall down.

When he scrambles back up to his feet, tears are running as freely from his eyes as blood flows from his nose. I ready myself for his next punch, but instead he rushes me with a full body tackle. I should have seen it coming. This guy is an ex-football player. I find myself smashed against my car again, only this time I can really feel it. I grab handfuls of his shirt and the two of us begin a brawler's dance. We keep this up for a couple of spins until my knee finds his chin.

As he slides off me, I notice the flashing blue lights of the patrol car. Judy Daniels saunters over. Her starched blue uniform has creases sharp enough to draw blood. Her sandy blonde hair is tied so securely in a ponytail behind her head, a single strand wouldn't dare come loose. She looks down at Keith. He's managed to get to his knees and is picking gravel out of his palms.

"Somebody want to tell me what this is all about?" she asks without taking her eyes off Keith.

"He stole my girl!" Keith bellows indignantly.

"You got any proof of that?" she asks bemused.

"Yeah," he replies, starting to cry in the pitiful way that only a large uncouth man can cry, "She told me so. She said she didn't love me no more. She said she was in love with him!"

He points an accusing finger at me and then doubles over and vomits. Judy waits patiently while he empties his stomach, then expertly leads him into the back of her patrol car. He immediately slumps over and starts snoring loudly. She checks the door to be sure it's locked securely before walking back to me.

"I thought he was dating that pretty black girl that works for you. Felicia?"

"He is, or rather, he was. They broke up."

"And now you're dating her?"

"Oh, come on!" I said defensively, "You didn't believe him, did you? Felicia is much younger than me."

"Under eighteen, if my memory serves me correctly."

"Yeah. Under eighteen. Too young for me. Now, she may have a crush on me, but this is the first I've heard about it."

"Speaking of crushes, what's going on with you and Mrs. Schmidt?"

"Connie? We're just good friends." I said, then I got wind of what she was doing, "Hey, what gives here? Why the third degree about my personal life?"

Judy laughs.

"Sorry, Randy. I've been talking to Kimmie and she gave me some ideas that are really none of my business."

I looked at Judy in confusion for a minute and then I remembered. Judy and Kimmie had a fling a few years back. I know you're shocked. Not that Judy is a lesbian too, but that she'd have anything to do with an irresponsible troublemaker like Kimmie. Judy saw Kimmie as a challenge and tried to encourage her grow up. Of course, it didn't take, but they parted amicably. They've stayed close friends ever since. Deep down, Judy still carries a torch for Kimmie and wants to see her happy. Kimmie must have told Judy about falling for Connie and about Connie spending time with me.

"Well, you flatter me, Judy," I said, "The way you make it sound, half the women in this town have a crush on me. I'm not that good looking, am I?"

"Actually, I always thought you had a cute ass, but you didn't hear that from me."

We share a good buddy to buddy laugh and then I look somberly at Keith's sleeping body.

"If you ask me," I said, nodding at the back seat of her patrol car, "I think Felicia told Keith that she was in love with me to get him to leave her alone."

"Sounds like something a girl her age would do." Judy agreed.

"And as for Connie, " I added, "I was talking to Kimmie about how sad it was for her to become a widow at such a young age and how we should all try to help her through this difficult time in her life."

I don't know why I'm making up all this shit for Judy's benefit. Even though I'm friends with Judy, she's still a cop and I sometimes get nervous around cops.

"That's very kind of you, Randy. Not everybody would take the time to do what you're doing."

Not if they had scruples.

"Well, Duane and I used to be so close. I feel it's the least for him."

"God bless you, Randy."

With that she climbs into her car and takes Keith to the police station.

CHAPTER THIRTEEN

I'm dragging my ass to the end of one of the most exhausting weeks I've ever experienced. The fact that it's early August of the muggiest, hottest summer I can ever remember doesn't help either. The restaurant has been swarming with overheated families looking for a quick meal and an escape from the heat. Mingling with them are teenagers with nowhere to go who have decided this is a good place to perform their awkward mating rituals, which seems to include setting our dumpster on fire at least once a week. Then I've got Mr. Bottenberg calling me from Feeler's Saloon every day with updates on how our plan to thwart Mrs. Bottenberg's desire to procreate with him is working out. And, if all this were not enough, I spend four days a week at Connie's, screwing our brains out, and the other three days with Filly doing the same thing. I have to get some rest soon or I'm going to drop dead.

What used to be my favorite time of the day has now become the most confusing. I'm referring to the drive home with Filly. We still have a great time talking about our day or anything else that comes up. But she has to suspect that I spend my business meetings with Connie doing more than discussing business. And I'm not quite sure where our relationship is headed.

Is Filly my girlfriend or just a fuck buddy? Keith claimed she told him that she was in love with me. Does she know Keith confronted me about this? Did she mean it or did she say it to get rid of Keith? And how do I feel about all this? Do I love her? Can I afford to love her? Do I try to find out where we both stand?

The answer is no. I can't afford to get into this. I'm too close. There's too many other distractions as it is. But even as I say this, part of me looks at her and still wants her. Part of me struggles not to reach over and grab her hand and tell her that she's worth more than a hundred Burger City franchises. Well, maybe she is, but right now, nothing in my life is worth more than one Burger City franchise. My Burger City franchise.

As I drop her off at her mobile home, her mother is waiting for her at the door. She's overweight and sour-faced with skin the color and texture of tree bark. She spits into the bushes beside the trailer and eyes me with disgust as Felicia bounces past her in through the door. Nice mother-in-law she would make. That sends a nasty evil shiver down my spine as I drive past the other sagging trailer homes to my place.

I go into bedroom and turn on the air conditioner. I sit on the edge of the bed and let the cool air blow directly into my face. I close my eyes and savor its delicious icy caress.

I can't do this for too long. Connie is expecting me over soon. She suggested I move in with her, but I was quick to remind her of how that would look to the community. I told her we'd have to wait until the proper time had passed and then we'd discuss it. Outside, I can hear a mocking bird complaining about how the lazy afternoon sun is making him too tired to hunt for insects. I should jump in the shower, but I decide to lay back and rest my eyes for just a minute.

A crack of thunder that sounds like it's in the room with me jolts me awake. The room is pitch black except for repeated flashes of lightning that illuminate the sheets of rain beating against the window. I'm groggy and disoriented. I glance at the illuminated clock on my beside table. It reads 10:32PM. I've been asleep for hours.

I start turning on some lights and then notice the message light blinking on my phone. Oh hell, Connie! Sure enough, all six of the messages are from her. On the first one she's slightly annoyed that I'm late, but by the sixth, she's in a total panic. How the hell did I sleep through the phone ringing six times? I dial her number and she picks up on the second ring.

"Connie?" I said into the receiver, "It's Randy. I'm so sorry. I was so tired I fell asleep and didn't hear the phone. If it weren't for this storm, I wouldn't have woken up until morning. Are you okay?"

"Oh Randy," she cried, "I was so worried. I almost called the police to start looking for you. I knew you wouldn't just not show up, so I... well, I don't know what I thought."

I know what she thought. She thought I had run off the rain slick road into a ditch and ended up like Duane.

"I'm fine, Connie. I'm sorry for making you so worried. You shouldn't be alone tonight. I'll hop in the car and be right over."

"No!" she shouted, naked fear in her voice, "Don't you dare get in your car. I'm just so relieved to hear you're okay. Stay right where you are. You must think I'm crazy, but please, just do as I ask."

"Okay, Connie. I'll stay right here and get lots of sleep. I'll come over tomorrow night and we can pick up where we left off."

"You mean," she giggled, "With the whipped cream and cherries?"

"You're a naughty girl, you know that, don't you?"

"Well then you'll just have to punish me." All worry is gone from her voice "I can sleep now. I'm going to go to bed so I can dream about your body. Goodnight, Randy."

"Goodnight, Connie."

I'm about to place the receiver down when I hear her voice again.

"Randy?"

"Yes, Connie?"

"I love you."

I'm struggling with my reply when she said, "Don't say anything. Not yet. I know that was a bit sudden. But after all the emotions I felt about you tonight, that's the one I ended up with. So, don't feel you have to say anything back. Not now. Think about it. I just couldn't let this evening past without letting you know how I feel about you."

I let a moment or two pass and then we exchange goodnights again before hanging up.

I put the phone down and go into the kitchen. I'm hungry after that long nap and I missed dinner. I grab some carrot sticks out of the refrigerator and munch on them while I take inventory of what food I have in the house that would make a reasonable meal. Outside, the rain is still coming down in buckets. It's cooled the air for now, but I know tomorrow will be even more humid than before thanks to all this added moisture. At first, I mistake the pounding on my door for thunder, but then I figure it out and go answer the door.

Standing on my front stoop, soaking wet, is Filly. The bare bulb above her head mixed with the raging storm behind her gives her an eerie glow. Her face is unreadable. Her clothes are plastered to her body and for an odd moment I admire her firm breasts and muscular thighs. But then, I come to my senses and hustle her inside. She steps into the living room and drips on the cheap carpet while I fetch her a dry towel.

She takes the towel I offer her and rubs it over herself.

"What's wrong, Filly? Did somebody hurt you? Keith? Your mother?"

"Be honest with me, Randy," she said. "How do you feel about me?"

"You know how I feel about you."

"No, I don't. And I don't think you know how I feel about you. I love you."

"You do?"

"I'm not some stupid kid with a crush on her boss. I really love you. And knowing that you're with her is killing me. Don't try to deny it. Whatever is going on between you and Mrs. Schmidt is more than just business."

What is this? Two women have proclaimed their love for me tonight. It's so unreal. Here I am trying like hell to avoid love so that I can get my Burger City franchise. Instead it attacks me from all directions.

But, on the other hand, I do have feelings for these women. I'm not made of stone. Besides, what good is having a Burger City franchise if I'm all alone. Isn't that why people fall in love in the first place. So that they won't have to live their lives alone?

Okay, so I want someone to share my life with. Which one? Connie is the safer bet. And she's got Duane's collection. But who am I fooling. I don't love Connie. Everything about me and Filly is wrong. But, I can't deny it. I want her and she says she wants me. I can't let this get away. I have to try and make this happen or else I'll never forgive myself.

I pull Filly roughly to me and kiss her. I mumble in her ear that I love her. I strip off her wet clothes and carry her to bed.

Afterwards, we lay on the twisted bedsheets and listen to the final retreating raindrops of the passing storm. I want to tell her everything about Connie, but I can't. When you try and explain the whole crazy scheme, it doesn't make sense to anyone except me. But if we're to be together, she needs to know some of it. Enough to trust me to make it to the end.

"I have been having sex with Connie."

I feel her body become tight with tension.

"Thank you for not lying."

"I don't love her. I never did. But I have to keep seeing her."

"Why?" she whines.

"I told you that I was working on a business deal with her. That's the truth. She has something I need and I have to screw her to get it."

"Damn, Randy. Keith is an idiot and he came up with excuses than that one. Maybe coming here was a big mistake."

She starts to get out of bed, but I grab her arm.

"Listen, Filly. You must believe me. Connie has something I want that's very valuable. But I can't come out and tell her that I want it or else she won't let me have it. So, I have to continue having this relationship with her until I can convince her to give it to me. I have to do it in such a way that she'll think it was her idea."

"Isn't that sort of like stealing from her?"

"Of course not! I'm not going to take it away from her without her knowledge. And I think I can get her to feel good about giving it to me as a... well, as a gift. Where's the harm in that?"

"And if you get this thing from her, you can sell it for enough money to get your Burger City franchise?"

"That's right." I said, feeling drained, "So, do you still want to be with me?"

"Randy, I'm a selfish woman in many ways. I don't like the idea of any man of mine being with any woman other than me. However, like I said before, I have ambition. Maybe that's why I'm attracted to you. You have ambition too. You're willing to be a little whore to get what you want."

"Hey. That's a bit harsh."

"Don't be upset. It was a compliment. But here's the thing. We're partners now. If fucking Mrs. Schmidt gets us where we need to go, then fuck Mrs. Schmidt. But if you don't come up with results soon, I'll kick your ass but good."

I wonder what I just got myself into. But I said too much. There's no backing out now.

"You got it partner."

CHAPTER FOURTEEN

The next morning when I get to work, I feel better than I had in years. I'm a new man. I figured everything out. It came to me in a dream. The perfect way to get Connie to hand Duane's collection over to me. Not only would she do it, she'd be tickled pink about it. In a very short period of time, my life is going to change completely and I'm going to be a new man.

And that's exactly what happened. My life changed completely, but not in the way I expected.

It was just after the lunch rush and I was sitting in my office catching up on some minor paper work. Lunch rush had been fairly light that day, but I still pitched in behind the counter. It gave me a lot of excuses to brush up against Filly. Each time sent a little sexual charge through my system. She would shoot me a quick grin and then act like nothing happened. So, I was feeling pretty good about the rest of the day being relatively light and low stress. I was a little worried about Connie. I had left two messages at work for her and she still hadn't returned my call. After our phone conversation last night, I thought sure she'd be eager for me to come by tonight. Oh well, maybe she got tied up.

I was thinking about calling her again when Kimmie burst into my office. She is crying. She is such a tough girl that I didn't know she was capable of producing tears.

"I'm sorry, Randy," she sobs.

I get a bad feeling in the pit of my stomach.

"About what, Kimmie?"

"I tried to stay away, but I couldn't."

"Please tell me this isn't about Connie."

Kimmie collapses into my guest chair.

"The heart wants what the heart wants. I went to her house last night. I wanted to tell her how I felt about her. She was really upset. She started to tell me why, but I told it didn't matter. I was there for her. She was really happy to see me. I love her smile. It just lights up a room."

I unlock my desk drawer and open it. There is my handgun. One squeeze of the trigger and my Kimmie obstacle goes away. What the hell am I thinking? I close the drawer and lock it.

"I'm almost too afraid to ask," I said. "What happened?"

"I won't go into detail," Kimmie said. "But it was the most amazing sex of my life. That woman is not straight. She is a full-blown lesbian."

"And you came here so you could rub it in my face?"

Kimmie looks hurt.

"No. We've been friends for too long for me to go behind your back. I wanted you to hear it from me. Connie and I are in love."

She flies out of my office before I can respond. Not that I had a response. I stand there, dumbfounded for a moment and then it dawns on me to call Connie as fast as I can. I make a desperate lunge for the telephone, but it starts ringing before I can reach it.

I angrily snatch up the receiver and bark into it, "Yeah, what do you want?"

At first, I can't even tell if the person on the other end of the line is speaking English. All I can make out is whimpering sounds and frantic sobs. Finally, I realize that it's Imogene from Feeler's Saloon.

"Imogene, what's wrong?"

"You have to get down here right away, Randy." she gets out between sobs, "It's Earl."

"Earl? What's wrong with Earl, Imogene?"

"He had another one of his fits. Only this time, it was a big one. Big enough to put him in the hospital."

"The hospital?"

"That's where I'm calling from, Randy. Earl had a stroke."

CHAPTER FIFTEEN

I hate hospitals, but then, who doesn't? You never go to one just for the fun of it. Everything they do to make it seem less intimidating just makes it worse. Scenting the antiseptic cleaners, putting the bright friendly colors around the cold metallic examination tools, gift shops with cutesy get-well cards and stuffed animals holding signs that say, "Hope your boo boo feels better soon!" None of it can mask the stench of worry that hangs in the air.

I find Imogene in the ER waiting room. She managed to throw on her street clothes before the ambulance arrived; so at least she didn't have to come down here in a sheer nightie and garter belt. Her eyes are red and puffy from crying. We share a long hug and then sit down in a couple of the puke green plastic chairs.

"This is all my fault, Randy. I should have known better. I shouldn't have let it happen."

"Whoa, whoa, hold on there, Imogene. Start from the beginning and tell me what happened."

"Well, me and Earl was sitting around drinking and swapping dirty jokes like we always do. Everybody at Feeler's has been so concerned about him lately that it became my official job to try and help him keep his mind off his troubles. Not that I minded one little bit. I love that man in ways he doesn't even know."

"Imogene, please."

"Oh yeah, sorry. Well, there we were and I'm thinking it's around that time that Earl usually wants me to do a table dance. But before I can get out of my chair, Lucy stops by our table and says howdy."

"Who's Lucy?"

"A new girl. Just started a couple of days ago. Nice girl. Big puffy black hair, dark complexion, dimples in her cheeks. Kind of heavy, but in all the right places, for now. In a few years, she'll probably plump up beyond where she can dance anymore. Hope she finds herself a husband before then."

She catches my frustrated stare and resumes her story.

"Well, for some reason, Earl decides that he wants her to do a table dance for him. Right away, I didn't feel like it was a good idea. Not that I'm jealous. But Feeler's is Lucy first job as a dancer. She's still learning the ropes and I'm not sure she can handle the table dance yet. Usually we have new girls start out dancing beside the table and then get up on it later. Well, I'm about to say no, but I can see Earl is not going to stand for that. He wants Lucy and he wants her on the table. So, I figured she's got to learn sooner or later, so I cross my fingers and watch her climb up there. The dance starts out perfect. Lucy's a fast learner. She's really pouring it on. And Earl is loving every second. I've never seen him look so happy. Then it happened. Earl has one of his attacks. I know we warned Lucy about it, but she didn't react in time. Instead, she topples over right on top of Earl's head. They hit the floor pretty hard. Knocked the wind out of Lucy. But Earl took the worse of it. At first, we thought maybe she'd just knocked him out, but then we realized it was much worse. We called the ambulance. The EMTs said he had a stroke."

Retelling the story takes a lot out of her. She excuses herself to go outside for a cigarette. It takes a good ten minutes to convince the hospital staff to tell me where Mr. Bottenberg is and an update on his condition. They point me in the direction of his room, but warn me that I'll only be allowed to see him for a couple of minutes. He suffered a cerebral hemorrhage and it will be awhile before they know how bad it is.

As I enter the room, a nurse is just finishing up checking his vital signs. I nod my head in his direction and she shrugs her shoulders. She leaves me alone with him. He looks terrible. There are all kinds of tubes and shit stuck into him. Poor Mr. Bottenberg. He's no saint, but he sure as hell doesn't deserve this crap. I'm shocked by how much it chokes me up to see him like this.

I pull my mind out of the dark well it's in and steady myself to leave. That's when I notice the heavy labored breathing and the smell of dead flowers soaked in molasses coming from the other side of the room. Mrs. Bottenberg has been in the room with me, for how long I can't guess. I should have felt the earth trembling from her footsteps, but I was too deep in my thoughts.

"Good afternoon, Mr. Crust," she said, losing all her R's somewhere in the folds of skin that swallowed her chin. "As touching as it is to see you here, I trust you made sufficient arrangements for someone to cover your position back at the restaurant?"

"Yes, Mrs. Bottenberg, I did," I lied. "Would you care to call the restaurant to confirm it?"

"No, I don't have time to do your job, Mr. Crust. You see, I have to concern myself with the welfare of my husband."

"Of course. Well, it's about time I checked in. I'm sorry about what happened to Mr. Bottenberg. I hope he gets better."

"I'm sure you are, Mr. Crust. You can go now."

I hustle out of there as fast as I can. Being that close to true evil always gives me the heebie jeebies. I make a beeline for the pay phones, only I don't call the restaurant. Instead, I dial Connie's work number again. She should be getting off soon and I want to catch her before she leaves. They tell me that she left early that day. So, I try her home number and get her answering machine. I can't stop now to worry about where she might be, so I move on. I give her machine the short version of what happened to Mr. Bottenberg and ask her to call me at home later tonight. Then, I call the restaurant and get Filly on the phone. I give her the same story I just gave Connie. She tells me she can either take a taxi home or wait for me to come by later and pick her up. It's my choice. I could really use her company on the drive home, so I ask her to wait. As we're saying our good-byes, I see Mrs. Bottenberg waddling in my direction.

"Is there any news on his condition?" I ask her hopefully.

"No, nothing yet, " she said, her face, a doughy mass of petulance. "We need to talk, Mister Crust. Sit."

Like a good dog, I seat myself in the waiting room. After a couple of careful passes, she manages to land her sizable bulk onto the couch across from me. She looks me over like I'm something unpleasant she coughed up at breakfast.

"We must consider the possibility that Earl may be too incapacitated to continue managing the day-to-day operations of our restaurants." she begins, a bubble of saliva escaping her lips, "Since I am part owner, that leaves the responsibility in my hands. Or did you forget that fact."

"No, of course not, Mrs. Bottenberg. I answer to you the same as I would to Mr. Bottenberg."

"Good. I didn't want there to be any confusion." she said, feeling warmer from the glow of respect she was forcing out of me, "And since I have no interest in running four restaurants, I see only one solution to this situation."

I can feel it coming. She can't wait to shock me with it, but I've already anticipated it. Just for the hell of it, I decide to beat her to the punch.

"So, of course, you would want Earl Jr. to take over for his father. After all, this is his inheritance. I know you wanted Earl Jr. to get his college degree. But I suppose at a time like this, sacrifices must be made for the good of the family."

Her wide-eyed stare of astonishment is priceless. Kissing her fat ass is not going to buy me any favors, but it's also not worth fighting her. You can never win against creatures of her sort. They've ruled the earth since the day they climbed out of the primordial ooze.

CHAPTER SIXTEEN

I drop Imogene off at Feeler's Saloon, then pick Filly up at Burger City. She's waiting at one of the outside tables and when she sees me she gives me a sad smile. She slides across the front seat of the car and into my arms. We hold each other without speaking for a few minutes. I fill her in on everything that's happened since that afternoon.

"Is Earl Jr. taking over a good thing or a bad thing?" she asks.

"Not just a bad thing, but the worst thing that could happen. Earl Jr. is his mother's child. He's fat, spoiled, and stupid. When he was little, he was one of those kids that likes to pull the legs off insects and he'll treat us the same way. He'll also run Mr. Bottenberg's business into the ground and blame everybody but himself for doing it."

"Why don't we just quit?"

"We could, but then we'd have to move and start all over again. I've got to stick it out here and see if I can't still make this Connie thing happen."

"I thought you had Mrs. Schmidt all set for you to make your move?"

I told her about my meeting with Kimmie in my office. Her eyes glazed over as I covered the more interesting details.

"You think this Kimmie can turn Mrs. Schmidt into a lesbian just like that?"

"She seems to think Connie is already a closet lesbian and that what they share is true love."

Filly puts her hand on my knee.

"Have you ever considered going over to Mrs. Schmidt's house and just taking these valuables you say she has?"

"I would if I wanted to go to jail. She'd know it was me right away. I'm telling you, my way is better. Nobody gets hurt."

"You sure about that?"

Something about this conversation was really bugging me, but I couldn't put it together in my mind. There were too many distractions. I had to drop it for now and think about it later. Right now, my main objective was to find Connie and convince her to give me Duane's collection as soon as possible.

Instead of going home, Filly comes over to my place. Much to my relief, there is a phone message from Connie. She heard about Mr. Bottenberg and is very concerned about how I'm doing. She promises to call me tonight as soon as she gets home. I stare at the phone, my brow knitted tightly.

"What's the problem, Randy? She said she'd call you later."

"Yeah...but two questions. First, how did she hear about Mr. Bottenberg? And second, where was she calling from? She left work early."

I dial her number rapidly and let it ring until the answering machine picks up. I leave a quick message that I was home now and expecting her call.

"She's still not home."

"Well, you could drive all over town looking for her or else you can sit your ass down and wait for her to call."

"Damn, I don't know if I can stand just waiting by the phone."

"Now you know what it feels like to be a girl." she said teasingly, "But I'll tell you what. I'll keep you company. How's that sound?"

"It sounds like the only good thing I've heard all day."

We spend the next hours with me surfing the web and her sitting on the couch watching my small portable television. But even the web can't contain my interest and I'm soon pacing the floors in a short track from living room to bedroom and back again. This irritates Filly because I keep passing between her and the TV.

Finally, she said, "Okay, that does it! This obviously calls for drastic measures. Come with me."

Dazedly, I let her take me by the hand and lead me into the bedroom. She has me sit on the edge of the bed and then removes my shoes, pants and underwear. Then she gives me the most amazing blow job I've ever had. It releases so much of the tension I've built up I can't hardly keep my eyes open.

"Don't worry, Randy. You go on to sleep." she said with a kind smile, "I'll stay up and listen for the phone. If it rings, I'll wake you up."

"Thanks, Filly. You're the best."

I lay down on the bed and fall into a deep sleep.

CHAPTER SEVENTEEN

I wake up. It's still dark outside, but I can smell dawn approaching. Filly is curled up on the couch, probably dreaming that she's still guarding the phone. I don't bother waking her until I'm ready to walk out the door.

"I don't think she called," Filly said, blinking the sleep from her eyes.

"There's no phone message either. I'll call her later from my office."

"You're leaving early."

"Yeah, I want to visit Mr. Bottenberg before I go in."

I give her a kiss and then leave.

As I steer my car into the hospital's parking lot, the sun still hasn't broken the horizon. A thick gray haze hangs over the sky as chirping birds select their early worms. Visiting hours won't start for a while but the staff is at the end of their late shift and just point me to the semi-private room that Mr. Bottenberg was moved to during the night. I slip quietly into the room and stand looking down at his sleeping form.

"Hey, Mr. Bottenberg," I said. "You're looking great."

"Call...m..m..me...Earllll." he croaks with his eyes still closed.

"You got it, Earl. Sorry I woke you up."

He shrugs it off. I can see in his eyes that he's happy to see me.

"You have to get better. Imogene is waiting for you."

"Wh..wh...what about Bu...Burger Ci-tyyy?"

Seeing how the paralysis of his left side is impairing his speech is killing me. Knowing there's nothing he can do about what I'm about to tell him doesn't make me feel too good either.

"Your wife is covering for you."

"She's going to fa...fa...fa...fuck you."

"She already has. She's putting Earl Jr. in charge."

"Bu...bu..Bitch!"

"Yeah, but she is part owner and Earl Jr. is your son."

"Er..Er...Earl Jr....not my son."

With deep painful effort, he raises an unsteady finger and jabs it into my chest.

"You...you my son."

He's crying now and I'm pretty damn close.

"You...my...son."

CHAPTER EIGHTEEN

I get to the restaurant with still enough time to warm up all the machines and have a quiet cup of coffee before the day shift shows up to prepare breakfast for the morning crowd. But it's not meant to be. Connie's car is sits alone in the parking lot with her sleeping inside. I tap on the window. She wakes up, sees me, and silently she follows me into the building. I lead her into my office and start my personal coffee pot as she sits down in the visitor's chair. The same chair where Kimmie proclaimed her love for Connie.

When the coffee's ready I pour us both a cup.

"You had me worried sick, Connie," I said. "Are you okay?"

"I'm not sure what I am," she said.

"What does that mean?"

"Please, Randy, let me tell it my way."

She breaths a dramatic sigh and sips her coffee. It's her show now. I'm just the audience.

"Yesterday was the strangest day of my entire life. I got up with all these plans to make a special evening for the two of us. I felt we had reached a turning point in our relationship. I told you I loved you and even though you didn't say it back, I felt deep down that you did and just couldn't say it yet. I was going to make us an extra special dinner and maybe do something for you that Duane always wanted me to do, but I never could do for him."

"I know I shouldn't interrupt, but I have to ask. What was it Duane always wanted you to do?"

"In Ray Gun Ray: Fastest Gun in the Universe, Ray Gun Ray's girlfriend, Big Bang Betty, goes undercover as a saloon girl. She's dressed in this metallic corset and her breasts are pushed way up high like two scoops of vanilla ice cream. Duane wanted to me to dress like that, you know, before we had sex. But I was too shy."

I smile at the image of her in that kind of outfit.

"Not to mention the time it would take to get you out of that corset."

She grins.

"I'm not shy with you, Randy. You make me feel proud of myself and my body. But, I'm getting away from what happened the other day. Well, here I was planning this big evening, so I wanted to get my work done so I could leave early and get everything prepared in time. I even told the guys that if I got any calls, not to put them through so that I wouldn't get slowed down. Those guys are great. They love me there. A lot more than they liked Duane, I'm afraid. Any who, we had that big storm and you didn't show up."

"And Kimmie showed up at your house instead of me," I said.

From the shocked look on her face it's obvious that Connie didn't know Kimmie came to see me.

"I'm still not sure how it happened," Connie said. "I'm not sorry it happened. But I'm not sure what it means. I feel like I'm a different person now."

"Was she better than me?"

"Randy, please."

"Does this mean...we're through?"

"I don't know."

I waited. I couldn't think of any way to play this round, so I just waited.

"I still have feelings for you, Randy. But this thing that happened with Kimmie. I don't know if it's something I've been keeping inside and didn't admit to myself. Or it may have just been one of those wild and crazy things you sometimes do in your life. You know what I mean? You do it once just for the thrill, but it doesn't mean anything."

"So, what now?"

"I need time, Randy. Time to think this thing over. Alone. Away from you and Kimmie. I'm not going into work today. I'm going to take myself out for the day and maybe do some shopping. Maybe I'll go see the new Ray Gun Ray movie. I'll call you tonight and let you know what I've decided," she said, then looked up shyly. "That is, if you still want anything to do with me?"

If you still have Duane's Ray Gun Ray toy collection in your house, you bet I do.

"Yes, Connie. I do. I love you. I'm ready to say it now. And when you're ready, I'll show you how much you mean to me."

She melts over that line. But then she pulls herself back together and quietly shuts the office door behind her as she leaves.

I can't decide who I want to slap harder, Connie or Kimmie. I flip a coin and it comes up Kimmie. It's a two-headed coin. Well, I can't sit here and fume. My future is hanging on Connie's decision this evening. If she picks Kimmie, she might still be willing to part with Duane's collection. But somehow, I doubt she'll want to have much to do with me at that point. On the other hand, if she chooses me, I'd be her man. And as her man, she'd assume we were going to get married soon. As her future husband, I could decide what to do with the collection. I could have it sold and reinvested in a Burger City franchise someplace on the other side of the country before she even realized that it was gone.

There's a tentative knock on my door and Tim, one of my day shift employees, pokes his head inside the office.

" Uh, sorry to bother you, Mr. Crust, but we kind of need your help."

"Sure, Tim," I said, "I'll be right out."

BURGER CITY BLUES

CHAPTER NINETEEN

The lunchtime crowd is heavier than usual. We're already short-handed because Filly doesn't show up for work. My women keep disappearing on me. I'm too busy to call her and we barely hang on to our sanity as we try to feed the endless parade of hungry people. Tempers are shortened by the delay caused by trying to please too many at once. Numerous cruel insults are hurled at us. Still we press on like Custer at Little Big Horn.

It finally lets up around two or two-thirty. I go back to my office and find Mrs. Bottenberg sitting at my desk, talking on the phone. She motions me to sit in the visitor's chair. I sit down, grateful to be off my feet at last. Finally, she hangs up and glares at me.

"The doctors are still not sure how much of his facilities Earl will be able to recover. With time and therapy, he may even be able to carry on something of a productive life. However, that means I am forced to take action now to ensure that everything he worked so hard for does not wither away."

She pauses to gloat at me for a moment. She's getting a kick out of torturing me. I don't think it's because of any dislike she has for me. It's just the one thing she's really good at.

"Earl Jr. will take over all of Earl's four restaurants tomorrow morning. You will assist him in whatever he needs. You will follow his orders without question. I'm not sure what sort of arrangement you had with Earl and I don't care. Earl is no longer your lord and master. Earl Jr. is. By the way, please remove any personal items from this office by the end of the day. I'm having it painted. Earl Jr. hates yellow."

After she lumbered out, I sat in the office that was mine until the end of the day. Fourteen years of hard work at this place. It was more my home than anywhere else I'd ever been. Hell, I even used to bring girls here after hours and do it on this desk. In fact, once when I was dating Kimmie...

Kimmie! I almost forgot about my good pal Kimmie. If it hadn't been for her, Connie wouldn't be out wandering the city trying to decide to whether to wear lace or flannel. Damn, that woman gives me a headache. Angrily, I pull unlock my desk drawer for the aspirin bottle and find myself staring at the handgun sitting there.

It's tempting, but who am I kidding? I'm not a killer. And I look terrible in stripes. On a quick impulse, I snatch the gun out of the drawer and put it in my back pocket. It was given to me by Earl Bottenberg and I'll be damned if I let Earl Jr. have it. Let the fat fucker get his own gun.

CHAPTER TWENTY

For the rest of the day, I play out every possible scenario I can think of to get myself out of this mess. I have to quit. There's no other way. I've come too far and done too much to put up with a day of the bullshit Earl Jr. and Mrs. Bottenberg have planned for me. At the end of today, I am out of here. But what about the franchise? I could still do it, if I can get my hands on Duane's collection. And that depends on Connie's decision tonight. If she chooses me, I'll still need about a month to make it all happen. I could move in with Connie during that time and not have to spend any of my own money.

But if she chooses Kimmie, then I say to hell with it. I clean out my bank account, put myself and Filly in the car and get the hell out of this lousy town. We'll start someplace new. But then what? My money will only take us far enough to get reestablished as a Burger City manager and a Burger City employee. We'll be right back where we started. Damn it, it's just not fair.

I clean out my office, through my former life in the trunk, and then drive to Feeler's Saloon. It's time Kimmie and I had a conversation. As I pull into the parking lot, I look for Kimmie's car and don't see it. All the same, I park my car and go inside. As soon as my eyes adjust to the darkness, I see Dixie sitting at the bar. She's very drunk and weaving to the point that it appears she and her stool are ready to part company at any moment. I rush over to her and grab her arm.

"Dixie, where's Kimmie?" I asked her, digging my nails into her skin.

She tries to pull away, but I hold on tight. Her eyes tell me that she's as pissed off as I am.

"Don't talk to me about that two-timing snake! She's stepped on my heart for the last time. It's reckoning time for that little sweet-talking bitch!"

She yanks her arm free from my grasp, the momentum causing her to start pin wheeling her arms for balance. I put my hand on the small of her back, giving her enough equilibrium to grab the bar with both hands and hang on tight. We both take a deep breath and let our tempers cool down.

"Look, Dixie, we shouldn't be fighting each other. I've got some pretty serious issues with Kimmie too. Let's help each other out. You tell me where she is and I'll go have it out with her. For both our sakes. Because right now, I don't think you're in any shape to deal with this. What do you say?"

Tears drive heavy black mascara down her cheeks. Her lip starts to wobble, but she's too proud to completely break down.

"That girl, Connie, called the bar and asked for Kimmie. Guess she knew this was the best place to find her. She said she was heading home and wanted Kimmie to meet her there. Kimmie told me all this. Said she was sorry but she was in love with Connie. Tossed me aside...again. Like I was old garbage."

"How long ago did Kimmie leave here?"

"I dunno, about an hour, hour and a half ago. I was kind of drunk when she got the call and then I spent the last hour making sure I was drunk all the way."

"Dixie, haven't you figured out that Kimmie is an idiot?"

"Yeah, I know. But she was my idiot."

CHAPTER TWENTY-ONE

The traffic is terrible and I try as many different shortcuts as I can think of to get to Connie's a little quicker. My life is hanging by so many thin frayed threads. I feel that at any moment they'll all snap and I'll fall forever into a black well.

I finally reach Connie's house and park my car behind Kimmie's. The sun's been down for a couple of hours now. There's lights on in the house, but I can't see anyone in the windows. Instead going to the front door, I walk around to the back of the house. I don't have any kind of a plan. I'm hoping against hope that something will present itself. And it does. I see Kimmie open the back door and step outside.

"Kimmie," I hiss at her, "We need to talk."

She throws her hands up in front of her and pushes her head into her shoulder.

"Please, Randy, don't do it."

"Do what? Put up with you screwing up my life! Why do you have to get in everybody's way? Why do you have to be such a pain in everybody's ass! Does it make you feel important? Does it give you a thrill? What is your freaking problem?"

"Please, Randy," she cries, "Please don't shoot me."

That's the first moment I realize that my gun is out of my pocket and pointing at her head. With the confusion of the day, I'd completely forgotten that I even had it with me. Somewhere the impulse had taken form in my reptilian brain and made the decision to take this action. Before I could think what to do next, I hear a new voice behind me.

"Put the gun down, Randy, nice and slow."

I arch my head around slowly and painfully. Standing behind me, feet square apart and holding her weapon in a rock steady two hand position is policewoman, Judy Daniels. Her eyes hold a cool calm lock on my abdomen. I pretend I'm one of those bad guys in the movies when they know they have to surrender. I gently move my fingers around the butt of the gun so that I'm holding it out away from the trigger. Then I very slowly bend down and place the gun on the grass.

Judy and I do a little tango with her leading and me backing up until she stands where I left the gun. Then she quickly scoops down and picks it up. She puts her own gun back in its holster and comes over to where I'm now standing next to Kimmie. She carries the gun loosely in her hand.

"All right, somebody want to tell me what that was all about?"

I look frantically at Kimmie, then back at Judy. I have no way of even beginning. Kimmie starts for me.

"Look, Judy, you might as well know everything.

Connie asked me to meet her. She was going to tell me who she wanted to be with. Me or Randy."

Judy raises an eyebrow, then gives us both a look that makes us blush despite ourselves. Then she looks at just Kimmie to continue her explanation.

"Well, I got here about the same time Connie did. We went inside together and that's when we discovered that she someone had broken into the house and robbed her."

The darkness of night hides the surprise on my face.

"Which one of you placed the 911 call?" asks Judy.

"Connie did." answers Kimmie, "I kind of figured they'd send you. This is part of your beat."

"Nice of you to remember," Judy said with a gentle smile. "Now, let's hear the rest of it."

"Well, we had a little time to wait for you to arrive. Connie told me what she had decided." Kimmie said. Her voice choked up. "She said it was Randy she was in love with."

Both of them look at me like I'm something really special. I don't feel very special at the moment.

"I know why you put that gun in my face, Randy." Kimmie said, "I'd have done the same thing. She's worth it. She's in there waiting for you. You better go to her now. She needs you."

"Go on home," Judy said, "I'll call you later."

With big wet tears in her eyes, Kimmie runs to her car and drives away. After she's out of sight, Judy turns back to me. She's holding the gun in her hand as if she's trying to guess it weight.

"You go along with her story?"

"Yeah," I said, "she told the truth."

"I really don't need a domestic quarrel on top of a robbery. Especially, if they don't have anything to do with each other." she said. "Do you have a license for this gun?"

"Yes, I do," I reply.

"You don't strike me as the type to own a gun, Randy. Why do you have this one."?

"Mr. Bottenberg bought me that gun," I said. "He insists that all his managers keep one as added security. Normally I keep it in a locked drawer in my office."

"Not a bad idea," she agrees. "Now, here's what I want you to do. I want you to put this gun right back in that drawer, nice and secure."

She hands the gun to me and I quickly make it disappear into my pocket.

"I want you to do it tonight. Right after you go and make sure Mrs. Schmidt is okay. Will you do that for me, Randy?'

"Yes, ma'am!"

I'm about to go inside when she grabs my shoulder.

She holds me steady and looks into my eyes.

"Understand something here, Randy. I'm doing this for two reasons. First, I feel like we're friends. And this looks like a friend of mine made a stupid mistake. I hate to see a friend throw his life away for a stupid mistake. Second, crazy as she is, I still carry deep feelings for Kimmie. I think I always will. This thing with Mrs. Schmidt has hurt her bad. She's going to need someone to help her through that hurt. It might as well be me. It may be rebound love, but it's something."

My underarms are soaking by now with the sweat of fear. I nod my head and try to blink the other sweat running from my eyebrows into my eyes. Inside we find Connie sitting on the couch, clutching a pillow tightly to her chest. As soon as she sees me, she leaps from her perch and throws her arms around me, suffocating me with joy. It takes me a couple of minutes to calm her down. Then, with her squeezing my arm painfully, we join Judy to tour the house and tally up the damages.

It's not as bad as it looks. Mainly, they made a big mess. It looks like whoever did this was looking for something, but never found it. Some jewelry is missing, but Connie claims she didn't own anything of real value. Finally, we reach Duane's den. Like the rest of the doors in the house, this one has been kicked in. We click on the light. The room is empty.

"They took Duane's collection," Connie whispers as if she were afraid the robbers were still around to hear her.

"What exactly did Duane collect, Mrs. Schmidt?" asks

Judy.

"Ray Gun Ray action figures."

"Did they have any monetary value?"

"I'm not sure." she replies and then turns to me. "What do you think they were worth, Randy?"

"I have no idea," I said.

But Connie knew I had already looked into it. I could see it in her eyes.

CHAPTER TWENTY-TWO

Judy puts a call into police headquarters asking them to send in the robbery squad. With a small nod of her head, she pulls me aside.

"Look, Randy," she said in a low voice, "Maybe you should go before the detectives get here."

"Why?" I ask confused and then I get really angry, "Hey, you don't think I did this, do you?"

"No, of course not." she said soothingly, "It's just you came over here, you know, very hot-headed, carrying a gun. Now I know it didn't have anything to do with the robbery and I'd like to keep it that way. Your presence here complicates matters. The best thing you can do for everybody's sake is to return that gun to where it belongs. Right now."

I feel immense relief from her words. At that moment, I wanted to be as far away from there as I could get. Thanks to Judy, all I have to do now is say good-bye to Connie. She doesn't have to know it's good-bye forever.

I find her sitting on the sofa in the living room with all the lights on. She's hugging her arms tight and doesn't stop hugging them even after I sit down beside her. Instead, she leans her weight onto my side and rests her head on my shoulder. The pressure hurts a little, but I don't mention it.

"Judy thinks I should go," I explain. "I'll call you later."

"You didn't have to do this, Randy," she said, her eyes staring straight ahead in a dull glare. "I'd have given it to you."

I look quickly around to make sure Judy isn't within earshot of our conversation. Luckily, she has stepped outside into the front yard to wait.

"Connie, how could you think I had anything to do with this?"

"Don't, Randy. I'm not as stupid as you think I am.", she said wearily. "You stole Duane's collection. You knew it was worth a lot of money. I mean, you did try to buy it from me. You probably didn't think I'd know how valuable it was. Either way, it's pretty obvious to me now that you seduced me just so you could figure out the best time to come here and take it."

It's moments like these that I begin to wonder what I did to piss God off so much that he would put me in this kind of situation.

"Okay, Connie," I said, "You're right. I wanted Duane's collection. With the money I could have made selling it, I would have gotten my Burger City franchise." Thinking about that lost opportunity, plus all the other shit I had endured makes me angry. I continued on with a rising wave of righteous indignation in my voice. "That's right, Connie, I would have. But now I can't because I didn't do this. Somebody else did. I don't know who, but it wasn't me. If I had, I certainly wouldn't have been stupid enough to come back to the scene of the crime and stick a gun in Kimmie's face!"

"Oh, come on, Randy. You can't fool me. You came back here just so nobody would think you did it. It had to be you, Randy. Nobody else knew about the collection but you and me. And as far as putting that gun in Kimmie's face..." she said, an odd smile on her face, "I've never had anybody do that for me before."

I look at that odd smile and try to figure out where she's going with all this. If she thought I had robbed her, why doesn't she tell Judy? What's more, she told Kimmie that she chose me after discovering she had been robbed.

"What the hell are you up to, Connie?" I ask.

"It wasn't hard for me to decide between you and Kimmie. As sweet as she is, Kimmie could never stay loyal to anybody for any length of time. I could never put up with that. As far as the sex went, I realized I liked it both ways. Maybe I'm one of those bisexuals. I don't know and I don't really care. What I do care about is having somebody around on a regular basis." Her odd smile was starting to make me squirm like a worm about to be hooked. "The way I see it, I got a guarantee that you'll be around all the time from now on. Being with me has got to be better than going to jail for robbery."

I feel all the air leave my body. She had my balls in a vice grip and was slowly applying the pressure. All she had to do was make the police think I had done it. By the time I could prove I didn't do it, I would be broke from legal fees and my business reputation would be ruined forever.

"Don't act so gloomy, Randy," she said and gave me an affectionate nudge, "I'll still make your favorite meals and treat you like a prince." Then she added with a girlish giggle. "Especially in bed!"

CHAPTER TWENTY-THREE

As I drive to Burger City, my palms are so wet with nervous sweat, I can't keep a firm grip on the steering wheel. I try wiping them on my pants leg, but it doesn't help. Plus, every time I touch my pants leg, I'm reminded of the gun sitting like a cold dead frog in my pocket that has to be returned to the desk drawer in my office.

But wait, it's not my office anymore. Earl Jr. is taking it over first thing in the morning. And since I have no intention of working for Earl Jr., I guess that means I don't work there anymore. I am, at this moment, a man without gainful employment. It feels oddly like freedom, though I know I'm a far cry from being free.

What hurts the most about Connie is the way she outsmarted me. All this time I thought of myself as a damn clever operator when it came to handling people. And then this silly cow comes along and takes me like I'm some kind of a backwoods country rube. It hurts my pride something deep.

I try not to think about Filly. I wonder why she didn't come in to work. She didn't even call in sick. I can't even begin to imagine about how she'll fit into this situation I've found myself in.

I need to go somewhere and get myself together. I decide to go by Burger City after all. Until tomorrow morning, it's still my home.

As I pull into the parking lot, I see the dumpster is on fire again. The kids that keep setting it on fire usually don't come around this late. When I step out of my car, I notice it doesn't smell the same either. Something's not right. I walk over to the dumpster, bracing myself against the searing heat and peer inside. That's when I identify the different smell. It's that distinct combination of scorched cardboard and melting plastic. Plus, the various dyes add their own extra aromas to make it a perfect bouquet of destroyed hopes and dreams.

It's Duane's Ray Gun Ray collection. Somebody has burned it all. I can still make out the Ray Gun Ray logo on some of the packages and a few of the figures are still intact enough to identify who they were supposed to represent when they were whole. I don't have to look for long to know it's beyond even considering any kind of salvage. It's all gone.

When I finally get tired of watching the plastic melt and bubble, I turn and walk to the service entrance of the restaurant. I'm about to put my key in the door, but then on impulse I decide to check and see if its unlocked. I turn the knob and give it a short gentle shove. It's not locked. With as steady a hand as I can muster at that moment, I slowly push the door open and carefully poke my head inside. Sitting on a high stool next to the food preparation station is Keith Fleeman. He has his back to the door so he doesn't notice me watching him. It wouldn't matter if he were facing me. His attention is tied up completely in the pile of burgers and fries he is devouring with animal intensity.

I quietly past behind him. In the hallway, I see a light coming from the half-open door of my ex-office. I stand against the wall next to the door and peek inside. Sitting at the desk is Filly. On the desk before her is a legal pad. On the pad, she is practicing writing my signature over and over again. To the side of the pad is my checkbook and some documents she must have taken from the desk drawers. The documents are related to restaurant business, but they have a good copy of my signature on them.

It's obvious to me what she's up to. She knows my account is heavy from saving for the franchise. Once she gets my signature right, she'll have Keith pretend to be me and cash my checks. She probably knows just the right places that won't bother asking for an I.D. I find it hard not to admire her ingenuity.

Her attention is wrapped up in the task she has set before her. She doesn't notice that I'm in the room with her until she hears the click of the door locking. We're alone now. Nobody can get in and she can't get out without going past me first.

"Looks like you stuck around just a little too long, Filly."

She doesn't flinch. Her only emotion is cool indifference.

"We would have been long gone but Keith insisted on feeding his face first."

"Well, since we're here, you want to tell me what this is all about."

She shrugs her shoulders. "I got tired of waiting on you to make your move. I had to make it for you. And when it didn't work out, I had to go to do something else."

"Plenty of money in there to keep Keith in burgers for the next couple of months," I said nodding at my checkbook by her side, "But you would have done better if you had been patient and stuck with me."

She shrugs again. "Maybe. Maybe not."

I leaned against wall next to the door and stared down hard at her.

"I have to know something. Why did you take the toys?"

A flicker of confusion passes through her eyes before she can cover it up.

"It was Keith's idea. He just grabbed them to be an asshole. I told him to burn them because I didn't want any evidence around to prove we'd been there." she said, then stared at me harshly. "Where were the valuables that you were going to liquidate for Mrs. Schmidt anyway? From the way you talked, I was certain they'd be in the house, but there wasn't a damn thing in there worth stealing."

I spit the words at her, "I was after the fucking toys. They were worth a fortune to all those geek collectors like Duane who spent their lives hoarding then. And then you and the chinless wonder come along and burn them! Tell me something, Felicia, how fucked up is that?"

"What's wrong, Randy? I'm not your little Filly

anymore?"

Our attention is distracted by the rattling of the door knob. I guess Keith has finally come up for air from his mountain of fast food. He bangs on the door impatiently.

"Hey, Felicia!" he yells through the door, "The door's locked! Let me in, damn it. This is not funny!"

We both ignore him. We have more business to discuss.

"I don't get it, Felicia," I said, "What do you see in this guy anyway?"

"Same thing I see in you, Randy," she replies, "He's a tool. All men are tools. You've seen my momma, haven't you?"

"Of course, I've seen your mother," I said, picturing the old wasted hag in my mind. "What does that have to do with anything?"

"All her life, my momma clung to one man after another. She gave them whatever they wanted, always hoping that they'd take care of her. Instead they took everything she had until she had nothing left to give. Now, look at her. All used up. Bitter and ugly. Well, I swore that would never happen to me. I was going to use men the same way they used my momma. Your problem is you ran out of things to give me."

This time I know exactly when I take the gun out of my pocket. I can distinctly feel its heft and weight in my hand. I can clearly see Felicia's face turn gray and the perspiration run down the sides of her cheeks. On reflex, she yanks open the desk drawer to make sure the gun in my hand really is the one that used to be in the drawer. Inside the drawer all she finds is a lonely bottle of aspirin. Outside the room, Keith's steady banging with his fist is causing the door to vibrate. His curses grow more frantic with impotent rage.

"Do you know what today is?" I said.

"Your birthday?"

"That's right. Thirty years old today."

"Well, happy fucking birthday."

I squeeze the trigger three times. One bullet blows a hole in her face. The other two hit her body, but I'm too distracted looking at the hole in her face to notice.

CHAPTER TWENTY-FOUR

From what I know of the law, if you catch somebody in your home or your place of business in the process of robbing you, you can shoot them dead. The old joke is that if you shoot the perpetrator outside, then drag them inside before the police arrive. Well, this was no problem with Filly. She was inside the restaurant when she shouldn't have been there. Killing her was entirely in my rights. However, Keith was another story.

When he heard the gunshots, he did the first smart thing in his life. He ran. He didn't wait to see who shot who or what the hell was going on. He just ran out of there as fast as he could. Since he was an ex-football player, he ran pretty good. However, since he was also seriously out of shape and had just finished eating a huge number of greasy hamburgers and greasier fries, he couldn't run very far. I caught up with him about four blocks from the restaurant. He was doubled over, gasping for breath. I thought he might drop dead right then and there. But I didn't want to take any chances and it felt too good to see the way the bullets made him do his little death dance.

I guess I could try carrying him back to the restaurant and claim I shot him there. But he's too damn heavy and I'm exhausted. Plus, I just can't see the point. Instead, I walk back to my car and say one last good-bye to the restaurant before I drive away. At the edge of town, I stop at an all-night diner with a sign in the window promising air-conditioning inside. The diner makes good on its promise and soon I'm savoring the cool air with a hot cup of coffee. I cradle it in my hands and hold it close to my face so that I can enjoy its strong aroma. There's only a couple of other customers in the place. Their minds are as preoccupied as mine. We're all little individual islands cut off from each other in this small ocean of Formica and plastic.

I'm thirty now. I have bullets left. I could kill myself. But I don't even have the ambition to do that. I guess I'll just sit here and wait to see what happens next. All I know for sure is that there will be no Burger City for me.

The End

ALSO BY ALLAN KEMP

The Black Phoenix
Hagar's Tears
Tales of the Black Phoenix: The Bitter Pill
Tales of the Black Phoenix: Panty Man
Tales of the Black Phoenix: Loopy in Love

You can follow Allan Kemp on Facebook, Twitter, and
Goodreads.

Twitter:
@theallankemp

Goodreads:
https://www.goodreads.com/author/dashboard

Facebook:

https://www.facebook.com/theallankemp/